About the

M. J. Allanson was born in Bury, Lancashire. She studied English and Philosophy at the University of Leeds and now lives in Yorkshire with her husband and children.

This is a work of fiction. Names, characters, businesses, places, events and incidents are either the products of the author's imagination or used in a fictitious manner. Any resemblance to actual persons, living or dead, or actual events is purely coincidental.

FERGAL'S WITCH

M.J.Allanson

FERGAL'S WITCH

Vanguard Press

VANGUARD

PAPERBACK © Copyright

2023

M.J.Allanson

The right of M.J.Allanson to be identified as author of this work has been asserted by her in accordance with the Copyright, Designs and Patents Act 1988.

All Rights Reserved

No reproduction, copy or transmission of this publication may be made without written permission.
No paragraph of this publication may be reproduced, copied or transmitted save with the written permission of the publisher, or in accordance with the provisions of the Copyright Act 1956 (as amended).

Any person who commits any unauthorised act in relation to this publication may be liable to criminal prosecution and civil claims for damages.

A CIP catalogue record for this title is available from the British Library.

ISBN 978-1-80016-491-8

*Vanguard Press is an imprint of
Pegasus Elliot MacKenzie Publishers Ltd.*
www.pegasuspublishers.com

First Published in 2023

**Vanguard Press
Sheraton House Castle Park
Cambridge England**

Printed & Bound in Great Britain

Dedication

For Nigel — my rock and the love of my life

Acknowledgements

To all those who believed in me

Prologue
November 1373

Though it was close to midnight, Thistlewick was lit brightly by the moon's rays radiating from the thick layers of crisp, white snow. It had not ceased for several days; falling in a relentless stream of icy masses. Each of the village's small residencies had been completely covered, rendering its inhabitants with inaccessible front doors and redundant windows. Most would not have wished to venture outside though, even if it was possible.

Such was the height of the snow drifts that the three determined men had each struggled to leave their homes, trudging as they were through knee-high slush, forcing each step to be a slow and laborious effort. This had been their chosen night, however, and it could wait no longer.

The falling snow bit at their faces and stuck to their hair and eyelashes in an unyielding determination to thwart their journey. Yet the men could not shield their eyes, no matter how tempting. The constant need to scan the skies for movement was far more crucial than blocking the unpleasant consequences of a winter blizzard.

Samuel felt the ground shaking beneath his feet once more, serving as a stark reminder of the necessity to the journey they were making. The tremor brought a fresh fortitude in each of the men to carry out the task, though they all hoped a peaceful resolution could be sought. They had been patient for many months and now the time had come to impose an ultimatum.

Peter's gaze never faltered from the dark skies above him, despite the torrent of frozen droplets hammering his wet face.

"Perhaps they have remained in shelter," he suggested.

"Perhaps," Matthew speculated, "although we must not be complacent for even a moment." He looked around him and listened for movement, taking his next step carefully. "I suspect the weather does not hinder them, my friend; devilish beings that they are. Keep your swords at the ready, and gentleman, keep your eyes open."

Peter nodded, gripping the handle of his sword tighter in his frozen hand.

Matthew looked at Samuel who remained silent. His steely gaze was focussed on the target in front of them, which dominated the horizon in its ghastly form.

"Nearly there," Matthew said reassuringly, tapping Samuel on the arm.

They trudged on, each step forcing their legs to push harder against the almost solid sheet of snow, but each step bringing them closer to the looming expanse of the manor house's giant structure.

"See there," Matthew said, encouragingly. "It is unguarded as promised. My brother would not let me down. I was certain he could convince the other guards to join him and he has not failed."

"And he will have left the doors unlocked?" Peter asked.

"That is what I asked of him." Matthew nodded, stepping on to the stone walkway. The snow had not settled here, such was the expanse of the entrance's extravagant archway.

The three men brushed off the snowflakes from their outer-garments and shook the wet from their hair. They each looked up at the colossal oak doorway, hinged with black wrought iron and bearing huge round door handles like oversized and mighty chain links.

Peter sighed deeply. Though desperate to end their turmoil, looking now at the manor's magnitude, brought forth the reality of the actions they needed to undertake.

"We are in agreement, are we not, that we will give him opportunity to speak?" he asked. "A confrontation such as this may inspire the honesty we require."

"We shall ask, of course," Matthew answered. "We seek the truth, not bloodshed, and whatever that truth might reveal, a plan can then be implemented."

That brought some comfort to Peter, although his unease was growing with each moment. "What of his wife and children?"

"They will not be touched!" Samuel snapped resolutely; the stern words leaving no uncertainty. His focus fell on Matthew. "It is out of the question. Whatever the outcome of our enquiry, no harm will come to them at our hands."

Matthew nodded his agreement. Looking again at the large doors of the manor house, he placed his fingers through the ring of one of the handles. He lifted the loop until it was level with his outstretched arm and then looked back at his companions.

"Are we ready, gentlemen?" he asked. "There will be no going back once I turn this handle."

The men looked at each other for confirmation, and took deep breaths before nodding. Matthew turned the curved lever clockwise and heard the latch click back. Using his weight to push against the heavy door, he stepped forwards and took his first look inside Thistlewick Manor, followed closely by Peter and Samuel.

"You cannot evade sleep forever, my dear," she whispered gently, kissing him on his forehead. She had been sitting by the crackling fire of his study but had felt a heaviness weighing in her eyes and had closed her book, setting it down on the table beside her. Her husband sat at his desk, staring at fragments of papers and stacks of leather-bound books. He had read each word of each volume, over and over, desperately searching for a solution.

There had been none; not even a hint towards an appeasement of their dire predicament.

"You must retire for the day, my lord," she implored. "You will be better rested."

He knew she was right, of course. His own eyes had never felt so heavy, but the desire to end their woes weighed heavier.

"You may go, my love," he whispered, kissing her hand. "I will follow shortly."

She smiled at the lie but was grateful for it. She longed for sleep and knew she could no longer keep him company in his search. She took her candle from the side table and left the cold room, longing for the warmth of her bed.

She made her way up the spiral staircase, shielding her candle's flame from the manor's many draughts. As she reached the final step, she could hear movement along the upper corridor. Her hands began to tremble and the flame of her candle danced with the movement, leaving an erratic and jittery shadow of her own image, cast along the stone wall. She blew out the tiny light as her heart pounded in her chest. She had known this day would come. They did not know the lengths to which her husband was going to find them protection. She had implored him to speak to his people but he had refused, adamant that he would find the remedy and restore peace. His people would not revolt, he had assured her.

The men crept along the extensive hallway, opening each closed door in turn in search of her husband. Flickers of moonlight shone through the small windows and she caught sight of their swords glimmering with each step they took. Tears flowed from her eyes. She looked back towards the staircase and wondered if she could remain concealed for long enough to return to the study, but the men were moving quickly. Before she could make her decision, she had been seen.

Matthew lurched towards her but Samuel held him back, giving him a reproachful look to remind him of his earlier words. Peter stepped towards her slowly, raising his hands in a gesture of peace, albeit marred by the presence of his sword.

"We mean you no harm, my lady," he declared. "We only come to speak to your husband."

Despite her wildly beating heart and quivering lips, she glared at him.

"And yet, you are all armed, Peter," she replied with disdain.

Peter looked at his companions, unsure of what to say. Matthew stepped forward again, slower this time to avoid alerting Samuel to any wrongful intentions.

"We are armed against the outside of the manor's walls, my lady. Not the inside. We could hardly journey here without weapons, as you know." He gestured to the windows as he made his reassuring speech, but she was not reassured. Their intentions could not be peaceful.

"Now, my lady," he continued more menacingly. "You will take us to your husband."

"No!" Samuel shouted at Matthew. "She will not." He turned to her and looked kindly on her shaking figure. "Please tell us where to find him, and then go to your children's chambers. Stay with them until we leave."

She glared at the intruders. Never in her life had she felt such animosity towards anyone, and the anger fought hard against her overwhelming terror. A sobbing escaped her as she feared she would never see her husband again. Far greater though, was the thought of leaving her children at the hands of these invaders and she made her choice.

"Where is he?" Matthew pressed. "Where is the king?"

She pointed to the staircase, told them they would find the study door open, and then began to run with all her might along the corridor, heading to the staircase which would lead to her children. She did not look back.

Peter reached the lower floor first, scanning along the corridor to see an open door. She had not lied. He approached the entrance carefully in case the man had been alerted to their presence. Peering in, it appeared he had not. He sat in his high-backed chair, holding a scroll of papers close to his face to read the words in the pitiful light of a single candle and a dying fire. Though it was not the first time Peter had seen the man, he suddenly appeared very small; a saddening frailty etched in his young features.

Matthew could feel the hesitation building in Peter's posture but he would not feel pity for the man before them. He barged passed Peter, holding up his sword as he strode towards the desk. The man looked up, seeing the sudden movement in the corner of his eye. A panic swept across his face as the three men entered the room and he dropped the papers onto the desk. He quickly picked up two small, leather-bound volumes and forced them into a drawer in his desk, before standing up with his hands held out to show he was not armed.

He shouted for his guards but Matthew laughed. He pushed the man back down into his chair and put his face so close to his he could hear the man's desperate breathing.

"They are not here," he sneered. "There is no one coming to your rescue, Your Majesty."

"Matthew!" Samuel scolded. "We are not here to be unpleasant."

Matthew looked at the king, seeing the fear in his eyes. He scanned the documents on the desk, taking in the sheer volume of papers and writings, wondering what the man was researching. There could surely be nothing more pressing than action in their current sorry state.

"We cannot continue like this," Samuel said to him. "You have had ample time to resolve the situation. All you need do is to tell us the truth and we will let her know. Where is he? Where is your brother?"

The man closed his eyes and sighed.

"I do not know," he replied.

Matthew leant into the man once more.

"I do not believe you."

"I am telling the truth," the king implored, "and have been doing so since the question was first asked. I do not know the whereabouts of my dear brother."

As he pleaded for the men to believe him, Peter opened the desk drawer where he had seen the man deposit two books. He pulled them out and began to thumb through the pages. They must have held a great importance to the man, he thought, for him to have tried to conceal them at such a moment.

Matthew continued his accusatory exchange with the king.

"I think you are telling untruths. I think you know exactly where he is, or rather, where his body lies," he declared. He was clearly enjoying the altercation. Samuel did not revel in watching the relish Matthew was displaying in his questioning. Whilst he agreed wholeheartedly that their actions had been forced upon them, the method behind those actions need not be merciless.

"Tell us where he is," Matthew shouted, losing patience with the conversation, but the man would not change his answer. "Then you must make way for your nephew. He will rule and this horror will end."

Peter read further through one of the little books he held in his hands, turning the pages frantically to take in the hand-written words.

Matthew held up his sword as the man tried to recoil in his unyielding chair.

"Please," the man pleaded. "If you kill me, my nephew will not rule. He is an infant, as well you know. His mother will govern. She will hold all the power in her evil hands and you will have given it to her."

"Rather that, than this," Matthew declared as he held the sword higher over his head, ready to force it into the man's chest.

Desperate, the king looked to the others.

"Samuel," he pleaded. "Samuel, please. You know I speak the truth. You would be giving the village to her."

His plea went unanswered as Matthew looked at Samuel. He glanced at Peter who was still reading and shook his head in disbelief. The man had never been able to stay focussed.

"Samuel will not intervene," Matthew snarled. "You know his daughter was the first victim of this. Why would he save you? You have done nothing to save your people."

"I am doing everything I can," the man shouted. He seemed more angry, than frightened, at such an accusation. He gestured to the desk, piled with books. "This is but a small section of the work I have been doing. I am seeking a resolution. Please. Just give me time."

"Books will not help!" Matthew shouted as he swept the piles of papers off the desk with his sword and they scattered across the room. "Lives are being lost and all because you wanted power for yourself. You had to kill him, did you not? He was a threat to your reign. If truth be told, he is the older brother and rightful king."

"I did not kill my brother!" the man shouted through tears. "He would not wish to be in power, I can assure you of that." But Matthew had grown impatient with his lies. He lifted his sword once again as the king sobbed into his hands.

"Wait!" Peter shouted, looking up from the book and hoping he was not too late. Matthew lifted the sword further, staring at the pitiful man. "Wait," Peter shouted again, lunging towards Matthew, "he did not kill him." He grabbed Matthew's hands and pulled him away from the frightened man. "He is telling the truth, Matthew."

The king breathed a sigh of relief. He looked at Peter, who was still holding the books, and nodded his gratitude. Peter handed one of the volumes to Matthew who began to read its contents, as the man looked on, relieved that the truth would finally be revealed. It took a few moments before Matthew looked up at him and sighed in a new found respect for the man before him.

As the king's hands gradually ceased their trembling, and his beating heart steadied its pace, he felt a sudden piercing through the flesh beneath his ear. The dagger's blade swiftly shot across his neck, as deep, red blood poured from his throat. He glanced up at his killer, seeing the loss of a beloved child in each of Samuel's tears. Knowing it would be the last thing he would ever see, he tried to convey his sorrow but he could not grasp breath enough to whisper a word. His head fell slowly forwards and his body slumped down in his chair.

Peter and Matthew stood in silence taking in the shocking scene before them. Samuel stared at his silver dagger, watching the blood dripping from its blade. He staggered back, smashing into the wall behind him and looked at the horrified faces of his company.

"Oh, Samuel," Peter cried, "what have you done?"

Matthew felt the book shaking in his hand and realised it was his own body quivering in a state of utter panic. He placed his sword on the desk and gripped the book in both hands, steadying his own unstable grasp, as he gathered his thoughts. Taking a deep breath, he handed the book to Peter and gestured to both volumes.

"Take these and destroy them," he ordered. "They must never be seen."

Peter nodded. He glanced towards the fire but could see the weak embers would not catch on the books. He would have to find another way. He hurried from the room as Matthew walked towards Samuel. Matthew took the dagger from his friend's shaking hands and wiped it on his dark cloak, handing it back to Samuel and clutching his hands in his.

"Samuel, please listen," he said gently to the shocked man. "We can still do what is best for all. Go now and find her. Let her know that her son can take his rightful place."

Samuel stared blankly at the king's body. Matthew shook him again, pleading with urgency. "Samuel, this is the only way. The events of tonight can only be justified if we end this. Go now and tell her. Be careful, but be hasty."

Samuel's eyes finally met those of Matthew. He seemed to understand and he, too, hurried from the room aware of the long journey ahead of him, leaving his friend alone in the study.

Matthew looked back at the king's body slumped crudely in his chair. If no good came of his death, they would be hanged for treason but he knew Samuel would not fail in getting his message to her and her son would reign. Peter would destroy the books leaving no written evidence to question the morality of their actions. All would be well.

There was, however, another soul who might be privy to the full truth behind their torturous existence. The king may well have confided in his wife; sharing with her the burdening secret forced upon him. Matthew would have to ensure she could not contradict their story, should the need arise. With a heavy heart, he picked up his sword from the desk, walked out of the study and climbed the spiral staircase that led to the upstairs corridor. He would follow the path of her earlier desperate run, and climb the upper staircase to her children's chambers.

She would have to be silenced.

April 1824

The lovely, spring day had started crisp and cold, but the early afternoon sun had cleared the chill, drying away the layer of glistening dew from the grassy land next to the river. A cloudless blue sky and warm breeze had inspired many of the residents to take to the open airs and enjoy a relaxing Sunday, before their duties began for another week.

Nancy sipped at her glass of iced tea as Florence straightened out their picnic blanket, where the wind had caught its corner.

"What lovely weather," Nancy declared, replacing a loose pin in her dark hair. "I do hope this continues into the week. The children at school are always far more agreeable when the sun is shining. Trying to teach them a thing in bad weather is an absolute headache."

"I can only imagine," Florence said. "It is quite true that everyone's character is instantly lifted on a fine day. My husband can be quite the handful if he has to work in the rain."

"Dear Angus," Nancy said sympathetically. "Although, he works underground, does he not?"

Florence laughed and nodded.

The ladies watched for a moment as three of the village children played catch with a worn cricket ball further along the river. The ground where they played was far wetter than the ladies' picnic area, and appeared really quite muddy. Nancy thought about their poor mothers trying to clean dirty shoes ready for the following school-day.

"Speaking of husbands, Nancy," Florence winked, "has your lovely young chap bestowed a ring on you yet? I am quite ready to be your maid of honour, my dear. It has been far too long."

Nancy sipped on her iced tea again and smiled.

"Luca is a frustratingly patient man, I'm afraid, and believes it is right to court for far too long before a betrothal." She leant closer in to Florence and whispered, "Although I do believe he may be planning to ask a certain question on the Easter weekend. He has already requested my company at the village fair next Sunday and I dare say he is rarely that formal."

Florence's face lit up and she squealed with delight, clapping her hands together excitedly.

"Oh, Nancy, I do hope so! Please, tell me the minute he asks!" Nancy smiled and nodded. "I wonder why he has taken so long," Florence pondered. "He clearly adores you."

Nancy laughed and set down her glass. "I firmly believe it is due to his dislike of my cat," she giggled, "although I do not think that bothers Weavles; she does not like him either. Or anyone else for that matter!" She stretched her legs out across the picnic blanket, leaning her head back to enjoy the warmth of the sun on her freckled face. "I do love it when we can enjoy the outdoors," she declared. "So much of our time is spent inside our little homes. The short days of winter leave so little freedom with the curfew, and the nights seem longer each year."

"Absolutely," Florence agreed, "and Angus insists on ensuring we are tucked safely in our homes at least one hour before darkness each day. One can hardly blame him though, after losing his sister at such a young age. He still blames himself for that. I can see it in his eyes when he speaks of her. I remind him each time that it was her silly idea to run to the barn at nightfall, but it makes no difference. He wishes he had been whisked away and not her."

"Oh, goodness! I remember hearing of it." Nancy reflected. "He cannot blame himself. We were children and we had never been told the reasons behind the curfew, merely that it was necessary. If we had all known the truth, those childish dares would not have seemed so tempting."

"If we had known the truth, Nancy, we would never have ventured outside at all. Our parents were giving us a little freedom, at least. I must confess to never truly feeling safe without a roof over my head. I doubt I am the only one."

The pair fell silent; each wondering if the children playing happily on the village green would be quite so carefree if they were aware of the horrifying reality their parents concealed. Florence looked up to the sky as a thickening of clouds floated idly by, blocking the sun and bringing with it a sudden chill. She sat up and looked towards the river as the calm waters flowed slowly past. Nancy saw Florence's expression change suddenly and her head turned quickly towards the children still practicing their throwing skills, and giggling with each catch. She stood up quickly, looking back at the river.

"Florence, are you quite well?" Nancy asked, seeing the panic in her friend's face. She stood up too, following Florence's gaze into the waters.

"Someone is in the river," Florence cried, running forwards towards the bank. "A child!"

Nancy scanned the flowing current but could see no sign of anything but murky water. She ran after Florence, desperately trying to see what her friend was speaking of. Florence kicked off her boots and quickly waded into the water, deeper and deeper, launching herself forwards until the water reached her stomach and she began swimming desperately against the current.

"Florence!" Nancy cried, knowing her friend could not swim well. She looked once again at the children. All three were still safely on the grass although they had halted their game and were looking on in confusion at the two women. "Florence!" She cried again, hoping her friend would turn back; certain there was nothing in the river but the flowing water, whose current seemed faster with each passing second. Her friend was clearly struggling to stay above water and Nancy knew she had no choice but to follow suit and bring her back to safety.

She hurried into the water, shocked at the force against her limbs as she fought the rushing surge and swam towards Florence's panicked splashing. She reached her quickly, and tucked her arm around Florence's chest, paddling back towards the bank with increasing effort.

Nancy felt an enormous relief when she felt the river bed under her feet. She pushed Florence ahead of her until her friend was finally able to stand in the water and wade through the muddy bank. Reaching the safety of the grassy edge, she gratefully collapsed on the dry ground. Nancy, too, tried to stand, but her feet caught on slimy vines, growing on the river bed. Unable to keep her balance, her arms flailed in the water as she tried to grasp a breath. With a sudden flood of water, she felt herself pulled further under the surface. She kicked her feet to free them from the vine's grasp and with a final desperate jolt, felt the vine snap across her ankle, allowing her to move her legs. But the new-found freedom of her limbs allowed the water's force to pull her away from the bank, dragging her under as she fought a futile battle against its mighty power.

Florence looked on hopelessly as she saw Nancy's hand reaching into the air one final time. Tears streamed down her cold cheeks, as she held her shivering hands to her face. Looking anxiously at the river's surface, she could see all signs of fraught splashing had disappeared. The ferocious current of the Thistlewick River had claimed Nancy's body as its own.

Chapter 1
March 1825

*"Go to sleep, Baby Joe,
No more tears must flow.
Time to rest, Baby Joe,
To Dreamland you must go."*

He woke in the armchair, again; the fire still burning in the grate, the well-stewed tea, now cold, still gripped in his hand. He ran his fingers through his beard and pushed his long, dark hair back off his face.

He looked down at his bare feet where his grumpy, black cat lay, stretched out, enjoying the heat from the crackling fire.

"I think it is about time for bed, Weavles. Come on old girl," he said as he stood up sleepily, yawning.

Weavles looked up at him, perplexed that this man kept issuing her with orders. She would, without doubt, do whatever she pleased. She was, after all, a cat. She chose not to move.

"No? Never mind then. I will have the bed to myself."

He stood up, taking his cold tea into the kitchen. He wondered if he should clear the sitting room table of the many discarded pots, but decided it would wait until morning. He was desperately tired after his day. His axe had seemed heavier with each tree he had felled and each log he had chopped down to size. He began to make his way up the rickety old stairs when a knock at the door startled him. He looked down at the old grandfather clock in his narrow hallway. Twenty past eleven. He must have been mistaken. No one would be out at this time; not after curfew. He took another few steps up, but there it was again. Louder this time, and far more forceful.

"What the…?"

He headed back down the stairs quickly, glancing out of the hallway window as he passed, looking for any signs of trouble. On his way to the door, he grabbed his pistol, which he had never fired, but kept in his home as law demanded.

As he unbolted the top of five locks on his thick wooden door, Weavles scarpered upstairs.

"Pussy!" he muttered, as he pulled back the last bolt and slowly opened the door enough to peer outside.

Squinting into the night, he could see the silhouette of a small man dressed in a smart dark jacket. As his eyes adjusted to the darkness outside, he could see the man's wavy blond hair, tied back neatly and a well-groomed beard. The smart jacket was adorned with shiny gold buttons on the shoulders and he carried both a steel sword, holstered to his hip and a small pistol, clutched in his hand.

He opened the door further.

"Danny? What in the world are you doing? It is well after curfew."

"My name is Sir Daniel, Luca, and I am well aware of the time."

Luca rolled his eyes and cocked his head at the small man, looking over his stature with an air of condescension.

"*Sir Daniel?!* We were in school together. I have seen you wet yourself and cry like a little girl. Why are you here?"

Daniel looked up at the skies nervously. His green eyes darted from Luca to the black starry night as he edged his way into the doorway. Though he clearly did not wish to be in the presence of his old acquaintance, he would rather that than be out in the open after dark.

"I am here by order of King William. He has requested your presence at Thistlewick Manor." He paused. Took a deep breath and looked up at Luca. "He is dying."

Luca towered over Sir Daniel, leant closer and whispered, "Might I suggest, then, that he request the presence of a doctor? I am, after all, a wood-cutter. What use would I be? The old cretin cannot even die sensibly."

The small man looked horrified. He had never encountered such disrespect regarding the king. He greatly admired the man, and as one of his trusted aids, would have gladly laid down his life to protect him. He stood to his full height, squared his shoulders back and in his most authoritative voice said,

"This is a royal order. You will accompany me to the manor house. And you must bring your pocket watch, the one with which you were found."

The ancient, stone manor loomed over Thistlewick like a mighty mountain in flat lands. Quite why such a small village required the colossal monstrosity was anyone's guess. Surrounded by eight feet tall stone walls and guarded constantly by armed soldiers, it was an impenetrable fortress.

Deep within the manor walls, in a windowless room, King William lay in his grand four-poster bed, each post adorned with emerald green, velvet curtains. Lit only by the ever-burning flames atop the many candelabras and the roaring fire that warmed the oak panelled room, the dark chamber had become the king's prison since age and illness had robbed him of his movement.

The royal physician stood by his bedside, lightly touching the king's wrist, monitoring his pulse. He reached out to feel his temple but the king wafted his hand away.

"I am still alive, Carter. Please leave me be."

He gestured to two of his guards.

"Help me out of this damned bed. I will not meet any of my people lying here." With painful effort, he sat up and swung his frail legs to the edge of the bed; his guards taking each arm and lifting him on to unsteady feet. Doctor Carter looked shocked but remained silent.

"I will sit by the fire. And I will have a goblet of wine, please, and one for my guest, when he arrives."

The guards led him slowly to a cosy armchair while his maid scurried to a side table and hurriedly poured two large goblets of deep, red wine from a crystal decanter. She placed them on the round table which sat between the king's armchair and the empty seat.

"A blanket, please, Martha, to cover these relics," he gestured to his legs and the maid tucked a large shawl around him. The king looked at her as she gently secured the cloth under his feet.

"No more tears, lovely Martha," he said lightly, stroking her hair. "Not long now." The comforting gesture only served to make the tears flow faster and she moved away quickly, hiding her face while King William smiled with a fatherly affection.

A few moments later, the arrival of Luca was announced by a sceptical guard and the large bedroom doors opened. The king requested that the occupants of his chamber leave as Luca and Sir Daniel stood in the doorway. Several of the armed men glanced at each other; reluctant to leave their sovereign unguarded, but the king would not be dissuaded. Sir Daniel nudged Luca into the room with his bony elbow and glared with a look that implored Luca to show some respect. Luca looked back at him, rolling his eyes but took a few paces further into the gloomy room.

The king looked fondly at Luca, though the sentiment was not reciprocated.

"Luca, my dear boy, I trust your journey here was uneventful, despite the hour?" King William enquired.

Luca nodded.

"It was, Your Majesty and thank you for sending such a powerful and imposing protector for me," he said, glancing at the wispy looking royal aid.

The satire was not lost on the king and he chuckled lightly.

"Sir Daniel is a loyal soldier, and rest assured, he may appear fragile but he is impressively quick with his weapon."

Luca looked back at Danny, grinning as he quietly mouthed, "Your wife says the same." Sir Daniel was about to retort when the king requested that he, too, must leave and ensure the doors were shut tight.

"Come, Luca. Please sit down. Have some wine," the king gestured.

Luca hesitantly took a seat; his huge frame dwarfing the tiny armchair. He took a sip of wine, not able to recall his last drink. It was, after all, forbidden by law. Sobriety was deemed essential for the village for reasons known only to the royal court.

A peaceful silence descended in the large, shadowy chamber while the king took a sip from his goblet and savoured the warmth it brought. He looked at Luca who sat awkwardly, clearly wishing to be elsewhere.

"It would be wise to sit comfortably," the king said, smiling. "It will be a long night."

Luca sighed failing to hide his contempt.

Chapter 2

"Their journey will begin soon. I can feel it," she declared, almost smiling. She ran her long black fingernails through her curly red hair with a look of pure satisfaction spreading across her features. Such an expression had rarely been witnessed on the stony face of Typhonia. Many of the women surrounding her looked unnerved by this new display of cheerful emotion. It failed to alarm Aeraki, however. She allowed nothing to frighten her, particularly the woman before her, whose presence she despised.

Aeraki perched on the edge of the altar, where few others would dare venture. It served as both the chosen bed of their leader and the monument upon which their offerings were made, but Aeraki's apathy to the forced grandeur led her to use it as a casual seat. She played absent-mindedly with her long, black hair, curling it around her finger, listening with contempt to Typhonia's proclamations. She glanced at the faces of the others, shaking her head at the absolute attention they gave to their leader, lapping up each of her words as they were.

"When the time comes, we will be ready, my lady," said Typhonia's closest companion, carried away by their head's jovial assertions.

"Of course we will, Kykie," Typhonia spat. Kykie bowed her head, regretting her speech. "We have waited far too long already," she continued. "This is our time now. No more shall we hide in this prison, picking on scraps we source at nightfall."

She stood, unfolding her enormous wings to their full span as the others cowered in corners, or shielded behind the withered pulpit.

"We are the Daughters of The Wind and we will rot no longer in these crumbling walls. Our powers will be seen and revered. They will bow down to us. You, my beautiful ladies, will be their princesses, and I will be their queen." A cacophony of howls and shrill laughter echoed around the dank, stone building. Typhonia savoured the applause of her audience but soon observed that Aeraki did not share their enthusiasm. She glided towards her.

"I will be queen, will I not, Aeraki?" she sneered at the raven-haired woman. Aeraki's blue eyes stared into those of her enemy. Her resolve did not falter but she begrudgingly replied,

"Of course, my lady."

"Good. I am glad, for your sake, that we agree," Typhonia continued. "For now, the sun has set on this day. Go now. Be free in this shielding darkness before the confining light returns and we must halt our hunting once more."

To this, there was no hesitation from the women. Each of the devilish creatures rose in turn, spreading their horned wings and launching their grey, naked figures into the night skies like a torrent of giant bats.

Aeraki stepped down slowly from the altar, sauntering

towards the bell-tower with neither haste nor urgency. She scowled back at Typhonia before opening her own wings and launching herself into the open air.

Chapter 3

"I can imagine what you think of me, Luca." The king stated. "You, of all the villagers, have always been able to see the wood for the trees. And I am not referring to your livelihood there."

Luca smiled at the attempt at a joke.

The king looked around him.

"Thistlewick Manor has stood here for over four hundred years and been home to six kings, myself included. The last stone was laid in 1372 as the workers completed the east wing. I imagine more would have been added if the first king of Thistlewick had lived longer, such was his apparent desire and obsession with the construction. It is a dreadful blight on the landscape, in my opinion, but contrary to rumours of my age, I had no influence on the architecture. Each stone serves its own purpose. Each room fulfils a very special function."

Luca raised his eyebrows and King William laughed.

"Have your say, Luca, by all means."

Luca stayed silent and took another sip of wine.

"Please," the king urged, "I am a dying man. This will be your only opportunity."

Luca looked hesitant still, but he let out a deep breath and began.

"I think this is a big old house for one little king, when the rest of the village's residents endure each changing season in tiny, wooden houses. This is less of a manor house and more of a fortified castle. You have ensured you are quite safe, while we remain afraid in our glorified sheds.

"I think for every ten logs I fell, it is a disgrace that nine must be supplied here. Is it essential for you to have each fire lit daily, while the rest of us freeze?

"I think that closing the doors on the Thistlewick Inn, and banning all drink was an appalling act of greed when you clearly have no shortage of wine and ale here. My house overlooks the old distillery and I see the lights on at night, hear the noises of the old apparatus whirring away. I see your men loading the carthorses each morning with barrel after barrel, and watch as they make their way to the manor.

"I think that I see Robert, Phillip and Angus heading towards the mines daily and working until their hands bleed and their backs ache. But then, the fruits of their labour are whisked away by your soldiers before their eyes have had time enough to adjust to the daylight.

"I think that I am looking, right now, at an old man who puts his own gluttonous desires above the basic needs of his people."

The king nodded.

"Yes, I suspected that is what you would think."

Luca was surprised at the nonchalant response, almost as much as he was at his own voice spurting out his darkest observations and cynical beliefs. The king laughed again.

"You are angry, Luca, and I would be too if I thought those things of a man in power. You are also bitter and I am sorry for that. Dear Nancy; taken so young and with so much of life ahead of her. I know you must miss her dreadfully. I too have lost people I have loved, sooner than I thought I deserved. I suspect your anger is exacerbated further with the happiness of your fellow villagers, unquestionably allowing me to act in such a way. That must be very vexing."

Still stunned and confused by the conversation, Luca nodded. He could not deny that the king was absolutely correct.

"Of course, truth be told, Luca, the villagers are obedient because they are overcome with gratitude. Everyone who has lived here, prior to your arrival, remembers how life used to be. And I assure you, Luca, those times were far from happy. I can tell you with absolute sincerity that everything I have done, each dark decision made with this regal responsibility, bestowed on me by birth, has been made with the safety of this village and its people at the forefront of my mind."

The king looked at Luca, trying to read his thoughts. He was certain the young man remained unconvinced.

"You brought the pocket watch, I trust?" the king asked. Luca reached into the pocket of his black overcoat and pulled out the golden watch. He saw the king's eyes light up as he handed it over.

"This, for example, always brought me much comfort." The king said turning the watch over in his shaking hands. "I am unsure as to why but its presence always had a calming effect on me. I kept it with me for eighteen years until the time came for me to return it to its rightful owner. Though it pained me to be without it, it was only right that it be with you." He handed the watch back.

Luca's expression did not change as he put it carefully back into his pocket, and the king laughed again. With that began a dreadful coughing from deep within his chest. It was the first time he had actually seemed like a dying man to Luca and a wave of sympathy flooded over him unexpectedly. The coughing lasted just moments but left the failing monarch frightened, increasingly aware of his own mortality.

"Oh! This silly, frail, old body of mine no longer seems to partner with the age of my mind. Not long now. You will have to trust me, Luca. It would appear that I will not have time left to tell the full sorry story; only what I need you to do for me and for the village."

The king began to cough again and was clearly frustrated at his body's determination to defy his wishes. He looked panicked as he leant forward and opened a tiny drawer hidden in the side of the elaborately decorated round table. His trembling hand pulled out a folded document, sealed with red wax.

"Take this," he said, handing the papers to Luca. "It has taken many years of work to gather this information. Take this back to your home and read every word carefully. I hope to goodness it makes some sense to you, for the sake of this village. I am confident these words and directions will guide you in what you need to do; or at least where to begin. Keep your pocket watch on you at all times. It will keep you safe."

Luca was dumbfounded; his face etched with surprise and bewilderment. He could not quite comprehend how he had gone from convincing his cat that it was bedtime at home, to being handed a secret pile of papers by the king himself in the privy chambers of Thistlewick Manor. A king who seemed increasingly terrified as he pleaded with a village wood-cutter to carry out a vital task.

"Take it, Luca, please. You must go now."

Luca held the papers in both hands, staring at the royal seal and wondering what secrets they held within.

"What is this?" he asked. "And why summon me, of all people?"

"This is your quest, Luca. You must do this because you are The Gift. I do not believe in coincidence. Your arrival dawned a new age for the village. There must be a reason for your presence in our lives and now is the time for that purpose to be revealed. Above all, though, you must, must find Peabody. You must listen to her and you must trust her. She is a vile creature, disgusting beyond imagination, but equally brilliant, wise and capable."

With that, through guttural coughs, the king called for his guards. The doors swung open and Luca was hurried out of the room. He looked back at the dying man, as he was ushered out by two angry looking soldiers. They seemed of the opinion that Luca had caused this sudden weakening of the king's health, and were not gentle in forcing him from the room. His last look at the man brought the unnerving image of a king besieged with anguish, pleading and imploring Luca to do as he was asked. As the irate guards closed the doors, Luca tried to see through them to the monarch, but was left in a deserted, grand hallway. Still holding the scroll of sealed papers, he looked up at the closed door in front of him, asking of no one in particular,

"Who in the world is Peabody?"

Chapter 4

Typhonia circled the nave of their ancient ruins. It was nearly sunrise, and yet not one of her colony had returned. She scanned the open skies above the bell-tower for signs of movement but nothing stirred. She ran her long, black fingernails through her wavy, red hair holding it away from her face with both hands at the back of her neck. Pacing back and forth she slammed her fists against her thighs.

Kykie worried too but said nothing, afraid of the reaction it may cause. Unable to hunt herself, she had been the reluctant, constant companion of Typhonia for many years. She had learnt that it was far safer to stay quiet.

"Where are they?" Typhonia yelled in sheer frustration. "There are just minutes of darkness remaining. They will all perish."

Kykie did not answer, but looked up to the skies alongside her leader, desperate to see her sisters returning. A terror ran through her. Not wholly at the thought of their loss but at imagining a life of solitude, left alone with Typhonia for the remainder of their pitiful existence. She wished she could fly up and view over the old cathedral's walls for any signs of her associates, but her last flight was long ago. Typhonia had rendered her a prisoner of her body as well as the treaty, in a particularly vicious rage;

tearing at one of her wings with her sharp teeth until it ripped from her back entirely. A long silver scar now ran from her shoulder blade to her hip.

Kykie could feel her heart beating rapidly as the skies above her lightened ever more. Her lips trembled and her hands shook. Typhonia, in a moment of clear panic, spread her large wings and propelled into the air, reaching the opening of the bell-tower in a matter of seconds.

"No!" Kykie cried, but saw that Typhonia was not about to breach the safety of the shadows. Her hands reached to take hold of the top remaining stone where once a glorious slate roof had stood proudly.

There was silence.

Seconds passed like hours as Typhonia manoeuvred her way along the rim of the tower looking desperately in every direction until she finally declared, "They have returned." Relief and anger swept over her in equal measures. She leapt down, landing gracefully on the hard floor and watched as each of the winged women descended into the shelter of darkness.

The vacuous ruins filled with echoes of flapping wings as the hunters returned. All but one.

Kykie looked up again at the open air, hoping to see one last form descending the bell tower, but there was no sign of movement above her.

"Where is Anemo?" she cried. The others ignored her, placing their spoils on the blood-stained altar, too afraid to answer. "Where is she?"

"Anemo is dead," replied Aeraki. As the tallest, and by far, most cunning of the sisters she had always dominated her peers and was not afraid to speak. Her blue eyes pierced through the shadows to her sobbing sister. Kykie screamed an unearthly cry, but the bearer of the news remained callously stern. "She flew too high. She had been warned before. We all tried to stop her but she thought she could out-whit this damned curse. She put us all in peril."

Kykie crumbled to the ground, sobbing, while the raven-haired harpy looked down in disdain. A grief overwhelmed her that her sisters could never comprehend. Anemo had been her only real ally, sharing a sense of morality lost on the others. Typhonia reached out to Kykie, cradling her head against her breast.

"There, there, little one. No tears, my dear. It is a huge loss, I know, and I feel it too. But it is also a great reminder that we must rid ourselves of this crippling treaty. We must lose no more lives. It will not be long now, I can assure you. Their *Gift*, their chosen son, will soon begin his journey. And when he does, we shall seize the opportunity."

Chapter 5

"Go to sleep, Baby Joe,
No more tears must flow.
Time to rest, Baby Joe,
To Dreamland you must go."

Daylight began to peak through the white drapes of the bedroom window. Weavles stretched out her front legs with her tail pushed into the air, nudging her pink nose into Luca's cheek; a subtle but persistent effort to rouse him from his slumber and feed her.

He opened one eye, still half-dreaming of the melodic tune that drifted through his sub-conscious every night. *Go to sleep, Baby Joe.*

Weavles prodded at his face again.

Both eyes open now, he looked around his room, his gaze falling on the still-sealed document handed to him just hours ago by the sovereign himself. Luca wondered if the old man had made it through the night.

He stroked Weavles who playfully batted at his calloused hand with her soft, white paw.

"Come on then, madam. It is breakfast time for both of us."

After quickly pulling on his black breeches and a dirty once-white shirt, Luca made his way sleepily downstairs, the cat weaving in-between his feet in an apparent attempt at feline murder.

"Oh, for goodness' sake, Weavles. You are an absolute liability. If I fell and died there would be no one to feed you, you know? Having said that, you would take one sniff, conclude I was fair game and chew my face off!"

"Lovely!" A sarcastic voice came from the sitting room.

Startled, Luca looked into the little room.

"Meredith, what the hell? You frightened the life out of me."

"Language, Luca."

"Sorry," Luca said, composing himself and giving the elderly lady a hug.

Meredith laughed. "Fear not, my darling. You are forgiven. I imagine you were not expecting me," she looked around the room, "given the state of the place."

"Sorry," he said again. It was quite a mess. He gathered some of the many pots from the table and began to head to the kitchen.

"No time for that, dear. Sit down," the old woman gently ordered. "Did King William call for you? He does not have much time left by all accounts."

"Yes," Luca said, puzzled as he sat in the armchair, under the small window. The old woman suddenly looked very grey and frail. "What is it?" Luca asked, concerned. "What is the matter?"

Meredith looked at him, tears glistening in her eyes.

"Oh, my darling, I knew this day would come."

"What day? What is going on? The king made no sense last night and now you are talking in riddles."

"He made no sense? Oh, he could not tell you. Did he give you the letters instead?"

"He gave me some papers. They are on my nightstand, upstairs. What is it, Meredith? Please tell me."

The old lady sighed and put her head in her hands. She had not wanted to be the bearer of this news to the man she regarded as her dear son, but the king must have been weaker than he had realised. She knew he had documented many details of the necessary task, but Luca deserved more. He should know the full truth of the matter.

She began the tale from the very beginning.

Four hundred and fifty years ago, two brothers, Fergal and Frederick became so angered by their father's doctrines that they journeyed away, hoping to begin new and freeing lives. They came across a dip in the valley, close to the waters but surrounded by mountains and forests. It was an ideal setting for their new beginning. They had acquired several followers on their journey and soon a cosy community was thriving in a land they called Thistlewick. They both served as governors of the quickly growing village and never regretted the decision they had made to leave their violent childhoods behind them.

Fergal, the older of the brothers, was an adventurer. He cared not for the day-to-day responsibilities and politics of the district. He loved to explore the vast woods and hills surrounding their peaceful haven and would often be gone for days, or even weeks. His diaries were filled with thrilling tales of his many journeys and numerous exciting encounters. He would write each detail with care before wandering away for more excitement.

Frederick, though, never felt truly safe from his father's overbearing power. Instead of a cosy, wooden cottage made a home by the others, he began to build a stone house at the edge of the village. He built room after room, constantly adding to the structure until an ugly and imposing fortress over-shadowed the land.

He was wholly dedicated to his duties towards the people of Thistlewick. And whilst his brother was away on yet another excursion, Frederick declared himself king. He pledged to protect the village from any harm, encouraged hard work and successful business, and that he and his queen would raise their children to nobility and secure autonomy against intruders. Frederick's diary told of no adventures, merely the deep fears that tortured his soul and the feeling of relative security that his ever-growing castle afforded him.

Throughout Frederick's rise to self-proclaimed sovereignty, Fergal had been notably absent. The villagers began to speculate as to his whereabouts. Though he often spent time away from Thistlewick it had never been for this length of time. One fine summer's day, a young lady, clearly heavy with child, came to the village asking, too, that very question. Where was Fergal? He had not visited her for many months and he was the father of her unborn child.

Her name was Magissa and she was a very beautiful young woman. She had long, dark, curly hair and deep brown eyes made darker still against her freckled fair skin.

She seemed kind to the villagers, at first, and they were sympathetic to her concerns though no one had known of her prior to her sudden arrival. Fergal had not once spoken of his secret beautiful love, as she was also a very powerful witch.

Magissa, along with many of the residents, did not believe King Frederick when he said his brother had left on his travels and simply not returned. Concern turned to anger within her. The heart-broken young woman vowed to curse the village with the spirits of the elements until her beloved Fergal was returned safely to her, or until her unborn child took the throne as rightful heir.

She returned to her cottage, deep in the forest and cast her spell, summoning Earth, Wind, Water and Fire to ravage Thistlewick.

Soon the ground beneath the small village would tremble with such ferocity; the villager's homes were all but destroyed. The rivers rose and flooded the lower areas, forcing entire families to hurriedly move to higher grounds, cramming into houses with family and friends. A great fire ripped through the farmland, destroying their crops and killing precious livestock.

But it was the wind that caused the most despair. It would swirl at high speeds, tearing through the village, taking with it everything in its path. The wind grew stronger each day until it was more than an element of nature. It took on life forms; evil daughters who would fly through the village, clawing at animals and children alike, stealing them away and feeding on their flesh.

While King Frederick insisted their fortunes would change, and anxiously dismissed the notion of magic, the villagers understandably disagreed. They were outraged at the king's apparent blindness to the tragedies tearing apart their community. Throughout their torment he appeared to have done nothing. Desperately seeking respite from the torture engulfing their lives, several of the villagers invaded the manor house. The royal guards had chosen not to intervene as the people searched the rooms for their cowardly monarch; they too had been dismayed by their master's lack of action. When they found him, cowering in his study and pleading for his life, they slit his throat, killed his family, and sent word to Magissa that her child could reign.

Soon enough the shaking ground ceased, the waters dried back to the river banks and a gentle rain put an end to the fires. But the Daughters of The Wind were strong. Though Magissa's powers had created them, the witch could not destroy them. Left with little choice, she made a mystical treaty with the element to restore some semblance of order — the villagers could live freely by day, and the harpies could fly at night. Anyone out after sunset would be vulnerable to their hunting, but any harpy out after sunrise would perish into the dust and breeze, from whence they came.

The new-born son of Fergal reigned for many years in the compromised peace of the Thistlewick Treaty, and this strange agreement lived on through his son and his son after that. Magissa's blood ran through their veins, and with that, came a magical protection.

The vile Daughters of the Wind would hunt at night, thirsty for human flesh but satisfied with woodland creatures and unfortunate wild animals. Before sunrise, each day, they would retire to their miserable existence in the old cathedral ruins beyond the river. But after centuries of forced limitations, their leader, Typhonia, grew tired of the constraints. Well aware that dark magic had given them life and then shackled them down, she sought another soul with witchcraft at their disposal. While the others hunted for food, she soared through the night skies in pursuit of a magical woman who could end their curse.

After many years of searching, she succeeded. Magissa's sister, Hazel, had spent her life living deep in the woods with her family. She had not practiced the craft with the same enthusiasm as her vengeful sister, but the power had been there nonetheless; a power she had passed on to her daughters and their daughters in turn.

One such great-great-great-granddaughter, Greta, was a very pretty but very lonely young lady. She lived in a stone cottage beneath the shadow of a great mountain, whiling away her days sculpting and painting, quite alone. She longed for company but knew her kind would not be welcomed in Thistlewick.

Typhonia befriended her, hiding her wings under long robes and visiting her each night with tales of life in the village. She told the impressionable young woman of an evil, despotic king who despised Greta's family. She blamed his hatred on an age-old feud from generations long gone. It was because of King William that Greta must live alone in her sorrowful solitude. The feud would last,

Typhonia embellished, until his blood-line reigned no more.

Greta grew angry at living a punishment she did not deserve. She travelled to Thistlewick, with dark intentions of ending the king's life, but the manor house was impermeable; a large stone wall surrounded it entirely. It was also heavily guarded by a constant presence of loyal soldiers.

Greta could not hope to get close enough to cast her spell, but she knew of a curse which could, at least, put an end to the bloodline. She climbed the giant mountain which over-shadowed her cottage, and from its peak, she could see the whole village, deep in the valley below.

It took several days of powerful incantations to beckon the malicious spirit she required. Once summoned, she set it free to infiltrate each and every resident of Thistlewick. The unsuspecting people would never see it, nor hear it or feel it, but from that day forward, no babies would ever be born again. No young lovers would be gifted with the joys of children, and of course, there would be no heir to the throne. Greta was thrilled with the effects of her alternative plan.

Typhonia, however, was overcome with anger. She had hoped for a far more immediate end to their hampered existence. She had, however, made a promise to Greta that she would end her solitude if Greta would end the reign of the bloodline. The lonely witch had, for all intents and purposes, fulfilled her part of the bargain and so Typhonia would do the same. Indeed, she ensured that a band of raucous and immoral hunters were informed of the exact location of a cottage in the woods where a pretty, young woman lived completely alone. So far away from anyone else, in fact, that no noise could be ever overheard — no matter how loud her cries.

After many years, and no heir, King William noted that the ground beneath him would tremble on occasion; a slight but undeniable shaking of the earth. The waters at the river's edge seemed higher each year, and small fires began appearing in the forests. The elements seemed to know that the well-protected bloodline was ending and the mortality of the king was a slowly decaying barrier to their fury. It pained him to know that he could not protect the village forever.

Early one morning, on a crisp spring day, the king walked through the village with his queen to greet their people. They took a long walk by the river, enjoying the pleasant weather, and a stroll by the edge of the woodland. Whilst the queen was admiring some budding snowdrops, the king was drawn to a nearby meadow by the sound of crying. There, in the tall grass, was a baby boy, wrapped in a dirty, fraying shawl. He lifted up the child, beckoned to the queen and looked about him for signs of anyone nearby. There was no one. Even the grass surrounding the infant was completely undisturbed.

The child was taken to Thistlewick Manor and cared for by the queen for several weeks. Within the layers of the shawl the baby had been found in, the king discovered a golden pocket watch which, from that day on, he kept on his person. It brought him a sense of peaceful comfort.

Within weeks of the discovery of this precious child came word to the king that several of the younger residents of Thistlewick were suddenly expectant mothers. Out of nowhere, it seemed, a whole new generation brought joy to the village. Alas, it was too late for the king and queen to be blessed with a child of their own, weary as they were in their aging bodies. The queen, overcome with sorrow, could no longer bring herself to care for the child who was not hers. Though she had grown very fond of the beautiful little boy, she asked the king to give him to a good home. Days later, she passed away; a broken heart blamed for her sudden death.

Whilst the king mourned his wife, he was joyful that the village appeared to be prospering. It had been a long time since any of the residents had enjoyed good fortune. He viewed the baby he had found in the meadow as a gift and somehow felt that the child was the key to ending their tiresome woes once and for all. He had entrusted the boy's upbringing to his good friend who, as headmistress of the village school, would raise and educate the boy with care and love. When the child came of age, the king returned to him the golden pocket watch he had lovingly kept safe.

For many years, King William felt that he had failed in a key duty of providing an heir, but looked constantly for other ways to serve his kingdom. Knowing that the elements were growing in wait of the day his bloodline ended, he sought to appease their appetite for destruction. He ensured that sufficient wooden logs were delivered daily to the manor and there, immersed within the cellar, where the grounds had been secretly excavated, a large fire was kept alive and burning; fuelled also with colossal volumes of alcohol made in the old village distillery each night.

To keep the ground tremors at bay, he ordered the miners to supply him with a hefty percentage of their daily spoils. Each precious mineral was then re-buried to feed the Spirit of the Earth. Though he had to keep the rivers flowing, a large dam had been constructed several miles from Thistlewick to minimize the rising levels. It could not completely hinder the sudden surges of ferocious currents, but it certainly prevented further disastrous flooding.

The Spirits of the Wind, however, would not be so easily satisfied, and to conquer that particular evil, every available resource was utilised to source a solution. His men were sent to search the woods and mountains for answers, bringing back tales of magical beings, maps to unknown treasures and countless legends told through the centuries of cures for such curses. The king had documented each snippet of hope, collated each promising encounter and kept record of each magical name, hoping that someday sense could be made of it all and the curse could be lifted.

The scroll of documents is the king's legacy, passed on to the one man he felt capable and worthy of such an undertaking.

"That man is you, Luca," Meredith said gently. "You were *The Gift*."

Silence filled the air as Luca digested Meredith's words; never before having felt such a sense of responsibility. His temper had been stoked with revelations of the rushing waters. He pondered the possibility that the curse may have contributed to the death of his beloved Nancy. He stood up quickly and darted up his rickety old stairs, avoiding his cat's bitter attempts to dismember him; she had still not had her promised breakfast.

He leant over his bed, snatched the sealed documents from his nightstand and rushed back down the stairs, searching for a sharp knife to break the royal seal.

"You have not even opened it!" Meredith cried in outrage.

"It was late," Luca retorted, cracking through the red wax and spreading the aged, yellowing papers across his sitting room's table. Laid out before them were pages of bizarre looking maps, strange verses, instructions and incantations.

Meredith's keen eye spotted a tiny piece of brown paper in amongst the pages and attached to a letter signed by the king.

Dearest Luca,

The parchment you see before you, was discovered, tucked within the workings of your pocket watch.

May it bring you some answers and lead you to the resolution of our predicament.

Faithfully, King William.

Meredith handed the message to Luca. He squinted at the minute writing, faded on the brittle paper.

Two lives, almost lost,
Stood together and won.
Their souls, now entwined,
Were gifted a son.
Their joy could not last
As they knew she would soar,
She'd hear of their fortune
And end it once more.
From high in the skies,
Came her ruthless attack.
I stifled your cries,
Trying not to look back.
I held you so tightly
But deep down I knew,
She'd find me and kill me
And then, kill you too.
I have left you alone,
The trees now your home,
But I must go now
To face her alone.
You were not left unloved,
My little Baby Joe,
But to keep you from her,
Your chance now to glow.

Phoebe.

"Phoebe," Luca said, sadly. "My mother, do you think?"

"That would be my thought, although we cannot be sure," Meredith said, shaking her head and reading the verse again. "Curious though, to sign it with her name."

"I have to find her," Luca declared.

Meredith took his hand in hers. "Luca, my darling, read her words. She sacrificed herself for you."

"We do not know that for certain. She may have survived such an attack, Meredith. Either way, I need to find out."

Meredith nodded. The king knew best. He always believed Luca would be their saviour and seeking the truth of his origin seemed a good place to begin.

"What else did King William say to you?" She asked.

"Just to trust someone called Peabody. Have you heard of her?"

Meredith shook her head.

"He said she was as ugly as a badger's backside, but brilliant nonetheless."

"Did he now? The king's words?" she quizzed, eyebrows raised and shaking her head.

"Well, perhaps not quite in those words."

The pair began rifling through the rest of the papers when a knock at the door startled them. They shared puzzled glances and quickly tidied the papers into a pile.

Opening the heavy wooden door, Luca sighed as his latest unannounced visitor stormed into his home.

"Danny, by all means, please do come in," he said with scorn.

"Sir Daniel," the small man corrected. "Meredith," he nodded to the old woman.

"Danny," she made a point of saying. He did not correct his former headmistress.

He looked at the small oak table and the pile of aged papers it contained.

"Luca, I do not know fully what the king has asked of you, nor do I know what your plan may be. However, I do know that Thistlewick is weakening by the day. Whatever your quest, I am coming with you."

Luca laughed. He stepped closer to the little soldier, towering over him with his huge frame. "At ease, Danny, you undersized runt. I do not need a shadow slowing me down."

"Luca!" Meredith scorned.

He stepped back but Sir Daniel followed.

"Listen to me, Luca, you massive half-wit," he ordered before giving Meredith an apologetic glance. "I am as fond of you as a thorn in my side, but I will not be dissuaded. I will accompany you, and we will be stronger together, than alone."

There was a pause as Luca searched his mind for reasons against this unwanted union. Other than a mutual dislike of each other stemming from their school days, he could find none and cursed himself.

Sir Daniel took another step forward but his voice had lost its anger. "I need to do this, Luca. My wife is with child and I need to know he will be born into a safe world, not this dire half-life we have always known. You know in your heart, whatever you think of me, I can offer assistance in your task. That can only be preferable to struggling alone. This pursuit of peace is too important to let pride hamper your progress."

The passion and resolve in Danny's speech impressed Luca. He said nothing but nodded. Meredith smiled. She reached out to Danny and Luca, taking each of them by the hand.

"Right then, my brave boys, you will need supplies."

Chapter 6

Typhonia glided to the ancient altar where the spoils of their hunting lay. She peered down her nose at the pitiful offerings strewn on the shrine: several field mice, four wood pigeons and a decrepit looking being that could once have passed for a fox.

"Vile cretins," she sighed. "We are dining on vermin again, I see!"

She ran her long fingernail down the tail of a tiny field mouse, picking the measly offering off the table, its body dangling down in a pathetic deathly display.

"Who is responsible for this?" she yelled. There was silence. "Which one of you saw this sorry creature scavenging the forest floor and deduced that it was an acceptable offering to your queen?" she shouted, her voice growing louder with each word. A small, blonde woman stepped forwards, hesitantly.

"I am, my lady. There was little choice this evening. The weather has taken a turn and the…"

"Silence!!" Typhonia shouted, hurling the dead rodent at the woman. It hit her in the cheek, splattering blood across her face, and slid down her naked body, landing next to her bare feet. "This is abhorrent, Thyella. How dare you lay this on my altar as your contribution? I am appalled."

The blonde woman hung her head, shamed by the humiliating scolding. She whispered an apology through quivering lips. Typhonia glared at her in disgust. She walked slowly towards the small woman, then quickly grabbed at her long hair, dragging her towards the altar. Thyella's feet tried to find the ground beneath them but Typhonia's movement was fast and she was dragged by her hair alone, pulling on her scalp in a burning pain. Typhonia pushed Thyella's face against the stone slab of the altar, forcing her features into the decaying wildlife that lay on its surface.

"You blame the weather for this?" Typhonia questioned. "We are the weather, you incompetent fool. I am exhausted by this. Night after night you fail to bring me any promising sustenance. After all I have done for you." She pushed Thyella's face harder into the stone top before finally letting go. She walked further along the altar, perusing the options before her and prodded a wood pigeon with her long talon, picking it up and sinking her fangs into its flesh. Still fresh, deep-red blood trickled down her face.

"You may dine, my ladies."

The winged women lurched forwards, pushing Thyella away from the table and grabbing at the dead creatures, sinking their teeth into the meat until just bones remained. All but Kykie, who loitered in the shadows, disgusted by the crude display and lack of compassion for their fallen sister, Anemo. She could hear their leader assuring the others that the king was fading. It would not be long, she promised, before they would be free to fly in daylight again, and a true feast would be had. Kykie closed her eyes and bowed her head, hoping Typhonia's proclamations were untrue.

Chapter 7

Sir Daniel and Luca, laden with pouches of food, flasks of fresh water, swords and pistols were suitably prepared for their journey. Luca tucked King William's papers, now neatly rolled and tied in a scroll, into the pocket of his overcoat. He gave Meredith a warm hug and asked her to look after Weavles as the unlikely comrades set off out of the village. They had never left its borders before and the journey before them brought with it a profound sense of unease. As they walked through the narrow streets, passing the small houses and pretty gardens, Luca explained all he knew about the Thistlewick curse, as Danny listened in disbelief. They had spent their lives obeying a curfew that no one ever dared speak of. From this alone, he had always known that the village held its secrets. But he had never imagined how dark those secrets were.

"Do we have a plan?" Sir Daniel asked, trying to keep pace with Luca's giant strides.

"Not really," Luca replied. He could see Danny was struggling to keep up with him, so he picked up his pace more so and shouted back at the small man. "We need to find a woman called Peabody. The map shows a river flowing between the mountains. If we head to the Thistlewick River and follow it upstream, hopefully it will lead us in the right direction."

"Peabody? What sort of name is that?" Sir Daniel asked, running alongside his unwilling companion.

Luca laughed. "I'm not sure, Danny, but she is supposed to be hideous so we have got that to look forward to. Hopefully, she will know where I came from and that secret will unleash some sort of path to eradicate this curse. Although, quite how, is beyond me."

It was now mid-morning and they had a long day ahead of them. Their clear objective was to journey as far as possible whilst also finding shelter before the sun went down, more conscious now than ever before, of the need to be indoors at nightfall. And so, they walked, and walked, and walked, stopping only for small snacks. They occasionally paused to look more closely if either of them spotted a shape in the forest that could be the home of the woman they sought. Each promising sight had been met with a disappointing boulder or mound of earth created over time by the ground's persistent tremors.

By late afternoon they were growing weary; the terrain around them appearing no different to that of hours ago. Only the river they followed had altered, widening slightly; the flowing waters seeming more aggressive by the minute. Sir Daniel stopped suddenly, peering ahead of them, where the river disappeared into the horizon.

"What is it?" Luca asked. "Have you seen something?"

"There," Danny said, pointing ahead. "There is some sort of outline across the river. A bridge, perhaps."

They walked on a little further, both men's gaze fixated on the structure as its form became clearer with each step. "It's a dam," Luca cried. "It must be the dam the king had built. Meredith was right."

As they got closer, they could see it was a colossal piece of architecture made from huge cut stones, each one twice Luca's height. The noise of the hindered water was deafening.

"Goodness," Luca shouted. "He did not wish to take any risks with this, did he? It's monstrous."

Sir Daniel nodded, shielding his eyes from the blinding sun as he gazed at the enormous structure.

"There's something on top of it," he yelled. "Do you see?"

Luca took a step back, peering up as far as he could. He thought he could make out something, an additional structure upon the main body of the building. "If we follow the dam around, there may be a way up."

Sure enough, to the side of the river, built into the stone, was a stairwell, spiralling upwards. They climbed each step slowly, their tired legs aching as they made their way to the apex. As they reached the top, the breeze blew against them but the air was fresh, the sun warming and the view across the land, breath-taking. The smaller structure they had seen from below was an enclosed building with tiny narrow windows and a slate roof. The heavy, wooden door was unlocked but the men struggled to pull it open, its hinges having seized from decades of neglect. With a final heave, it flew open, knocking the men backwards into the surrounding stone barricade.

The building's contents were scarce: a couple of benches and a small table but it was sheltered and the two men agreed they should end their travels for the day and retire in its sturdy walls. The sun was fading behind the mountains as they ate sweetbreads and drank their water. Luca secured the door, wedging his sword through the rusted bolt and the men lay in make-shift beds, waiting for darkness.

"Congratulations, Danny," Luca said, sleepily. "I did not say it before, but congratulations."

"Sorry?" Danny queried.

"You and your wife are expecting a child. It is wonderful news. I am really pleased for you both."

Sir Daniel waited for the sarcasm to follow, but none came and Luca seemed genuinely sincere.

"Thank you, Luca. That means a great deal, coming from you."

Luca nodded, surprised by his own words.

Danny sat up, leaning against the wall and looked at Luca.

"I know you dislike me, Luca, and I cannot blame you for that. My behaviour towards you in school was absolutely uncalled for. I should never have said you were an unwanted child. I know I made life very difficult for you, and for that, I am truly sorry."

"*Unwanted?* Is that how you remember it?" Luca asked, not expecting a reply. "You told the entire school that I was such an ugly baby my parents had left me in a pigsty to be raised by hogs." Danny's face flushed with shame.

"I am so sorry, Luca. I could not have been more wrong, and I am not just referring to knowing now that you were not abandoned. I mean you are far from ugly. I was jealous of you, if truth be told. The girls all had eyes for you; never for me."

"And yet, of the two of us, you are the married man, here, Danny. You have succeeded there, where I have failed."

Danny shook his head and said gently, "Nancy would have married you in a heartbeat, you know that." Luca looked at the floor, twisting his flask around in his hands thoughtlessly. Danny was unsure whether to speak further on the matter, but thought Luca ought to be told something and now seemed as good a time as ever. "I have spoken to poor Angus many times since that day, Luca. Florence still weeps each night for her closest friend. He holds her tightly in his arms until she sleeps, heartbroken at what she has become."

"At least he gets to hold her in his arms." Luca snapped. "I have no one there to stop my tears." He slammed his flask onto the floor and stood up, looking out of one of the narrow windows at the river below. "What was she thinking, going into the water like that?" he asked. "Everyone knows the current is far stronger than it appears."

Danny could feel the anger radiating from Luca and felt a deep sorrow for his loss, knowing how much his own wife meant to him and the joy she brought to his life. "Florence is adamant that she saw a child in the water that day, Luca. At least, she was absolutely insistent on that, when she still spoke. It has been many months now since she has uttered a word, but soon after the tragedy, she had said it looked to be a little girl with blonde hair and a white nightdress. She was certain the child was drowning. She cannot be blamed for trying to save a little girl. Anyone would do the same."

Luca turned abruptly to face Danny, angered at his falsely placed defence of the woman. "There was no one in the water, Danny. No one else saw a thing, and there was more than one witness to the event. The woman is quite mad and Nancy paid the price for Florence's distorted visions."

"She was not mad prior to the tragedy, Luca. Her ceaseless memory of that day has led her to that. She lives now in a constant state of confusion, reliving in her mind every moment that led to the event. Her guilt is overwhelming."

"It is more than she deserves." Luca stated bluntly as he sat back down on his overcoat.

An awkward silence fell between them. Danny thought, perhaps, he should not have raised the issue, but he felt a dreadful sorrow for Angus. Florence had become a vacant shell of a woman, trapped in her own catatonic misery, and it was truly heart-breaking to observe. However, it was Angus who lived each day with the haunted vessel, resembling the woman he once loved, but so far removed from the essence of her, she was but a stranger to him now.

"There was a little girl," she would say, over and over as she stared from her bedroom window at the flowing river. Angus would agree with her to pacify her guilt and rouse her spirits, but she would continue to look out, as if

seeing the child again would somehow vindicate the events of that fateful day. After months, he stopped agreeing and left her to stare, continuing his daily life as best he could.

Not wishing to discuss this further, Luca changed the subject. "I wonder what this is for," he said, gesturing around him to their abode for the night.

"Some sort of observation centre?" Danny suggested, glad now that the discussion had ended, and sorry he had opened up the conversation. "Perhaps someone was posted here to check the river would not breach the sides."

"So why would they build such narrow windows?" Luca asked. "You can barely see the river. Any wintery weather would force a man inside and be left blind to the dam's success or failure." Even as he said it, a realisation washed over Luca. "It is not for the river, Danny. This is to view the harpies!!"

Danny's face went white. Knowing now that the legends were true, the thought of seeing one was absolutely horrifying.

Luca took the scroll of papers from his pocket. He opened it out on the floor and searched through the maps by the dim light of a single candle.

"Look, there," he pointed to the map, showing Danny the vague drawings and scrawled writing. He traced his finger along the images on the paper. "Here is the river, this must be the dam and here, just over the mountain, there is a church, by the look of it." Luca squinted at the small drawing. Next to the image was written a single word.

Lair.

"Good lord!" Danny said.

Chapter 8

The dank cathedral walls grew darker. Seven seemingly lifeless winged forms lay in the centre of the large room, their limbs entangled in their pit. Typhonia's hellish form lay strewn across the reddened stone altar, Kykie sleeping at her feet, curled in a ball like a gruesome pet, her one wing enclosing her frame.

It was Aeraki who rose first; the raven-haired beauty with piercing blue eyes. She stood and stretched her giant wings, looking at her sisters with callous scorn. She could see Typhonia's still figure on the altar — her pathetic puppy asleep at her feet.

The others began to stir as Aeraki strode to the altar, gently rousing her leader, restraining the urge to do her harm.

"The darkness comes, my lady," she whispered.

"Good," her queen responded, her eyes still shut. She slowly rose, startling Kykie who scuttled off the altar and crouched behind a pillar. Typhonia looked at the skies above them. It was the purest black.

"It is our time, once more, my beautiful ladies. Take to the skies. Return safely bearing goods worthy of a place at our altar."

Seven winged women shot into the skies like monstrous eagles; their large wings beating in unison as they soared over the mountain.

Visible only against the night sky by the light of the crescent moon, they flew quickly, their eyes searching the grounds beneath them for any movement.

Chapter 9

Luca blew out the candle, fearing its faint glow could spark unwanted curiosity in the abandoned building. The men took a window each to watch for signs of their feared enemy, knowing the darkness would draw them out. It did not take long.

"There, I see them," Luca said. Danny rushed over. They stood in silence, their eyes beholding an unearthly sight.

Each creature was a devilish form. Each had wings as wide as they were tall.

Five of the airborne women flew towards Thistlewick but two of them decided on a different hunting ground, coasting along the river towards the men's lodgings. Luca could feel Danny trembling next to him as the forms became clearer, but the small man reached for his pistol with calm resolve. Luca followed suit, hoping it would not be needed. They looked on as the women landed in the forest canopy, picking through the branches and sniffing the air in search of animal scents. Clearly unimpressed by their current position, the women rose once more into the air, flying closer still to the dam.

"What is that scent?" Aeraki questioned as she stood on the branches of a large oak tree, her nostrils flaring at the unfamiliar smell she had detected in the air. Thyella breathed in hard, tracing the odour too. Within seconds the harpies landed on the slate roof of the observation centre, knocking several tiles to the ground. Luca heard them smash beneath the window as the men crouched down, staying as still and as quiet as they could.

"I think we have some company," Aeraki sang in a sickening melody. Luca heard the other harpy laughing, as loud footsteps rattled across the roof. Danny gripped his pistol tighter, seeking out the trigger with his shaking fingers.

"Thyella, look, I spy a door. Our feast is beckoning us in," Aeraki shrilled, "and we are not in the village now so we can enter as we please." Her blonde sister instantly flew towards the entrance way, clawing at the handle. Luca lurched towards the door, not trusting his rudimentary lock, though the solid steel sword held fast. Danny stood with his back tight against the wall, his pistol pointing at the windows though he knew they would be far too narrow for entrance. A movement to his right caught his eye and he peered through the window beside him. Two piercing blue eyes stared back.

Aeraki's talons shot through the thick glass, and within a second, her strong fingers gripped Danny's throat. As her claws dug in to his neck, breaking his flesh, Danny's pistol dropped from his grip, clattering across the floor and bouncing out of reach.

Luca leapt across the room, grabbing Danny's sword from beside the table, his own still bolting shut the heavy door. Danny gripped Aeraki's arm, desperately trying to force away her vice-like hold. She laughed menacingly, shouting to her sister that they would be dining well tonight. Absorbed in her arrogant jibing, she did not see as Luca swung the sword down hard on her arm, missing Danny's panicking hands by a margin. Her sickening laugh turned into a panicked scream as her arm recoiled at the elbow, and they heard her slump to the ground outside. Her severed and bloody hand dropped to the floor next to Danny as Luca's swing cut clean through the flesh and bone. The men watched in horrified silence as the dismembered limb crackled and withered before their eyes, leaving behind it an animalistic, skeletal claw.

Luca aimed his pistol through the broken glass of the narrow window. The moment he saw movement outside, he fired. He knew he had hit the raven-haired harpy instantly. Her flight became erratic until she could continue no longer and succumbed to the wound, plunging from the sky. Her sister caught hold of her flailing body before she crashed into the water. She carried her high into the air, disappearing over the mountain top.

Danny sighed with relief. He felt his neck for wounds but noted only scratches.

"You got her! Well done," he cried, tapping Luca on the arm. Luca did not look quite so relieved.

"They will be back, Danny, and there will be more of them. We have to leave this place. We have to go now!"

"Go out there? Are you mad? They cannot get in here. Out there we are completely open to their assault."

"Two of them nearly got in, Danny. Seven of the flying bitches definitely will." He looked towards the door. "That sword is solid but you can see the bolt is rusty and brittle. Even if that holds them at bay, they need only set fire to the door itself and smoke us out."

That thought had not occurred to Danny. With that, he agreed. Better to be on the run than trapped and helpless under attack. They gathered their belongings quickly, pulled the sword from the bolt and darted down the spiralling stairs, running towards the forest for cover.

Thyella clutched Aeraki's body, moving quickly through the night sky, back to the safety of the crumbling cathedral. She flew through the open roof space of the old bell-tower and gently placed Aeraki on the altar.

Typhonia and Kykie were quickly by her side, licking at their sister's wounds. Aeraki writhed in agony but grew stronger with each touch from her queen and fellow harpies.

"You have been injured by a human. They were out after curfew?" Typhonia asked.

"Two men, my lady, armed, as you can see," Thyella interjected. "They were holed up in the old dam house."

Typhonia grinned, bearing her sharp teeth with a look of evil glee.

"This is good news," she said. "Go now, Thyella. Fear not for your sister. We will take care of her. Gather the others and do not return without these mortals."

Thyella flew off quickly, knowing Kykie would not rest until Aeraki was well; such was her nature despite Aeraki's temperament.

She made her way towards Thistlewick excitedly.

News of human prey would delight her sisters and the thought of revealing this good fortune was almost as enticing as the thought of dining on their bodies.

Chapter 10

The men moved quickly through the dense trees, desperately searching for some sort of cover. There were hours left of darkness and they needed safety urgently.

"Was there anything else on the map nearby?" Danny shouted as his legs powered on, keeping up with Luca.

"Just loads of bloody trees," Luca shouted back.

"Six," Danny shouted.

"What?"

"There would be six of them flying back. You just killed one."

"If it was that easy, my friend, they would have been wiped out long ago. And we do not know how many more of them might have stayed behind. There could be hundreds of the things."

"Damn!" Danny muttered. This awful hypothesis spurred on his legs to pump harder and faster. "What the hell is that smell?"

"I don't know, but I can smell it too. It seems to be getting stronger."

"Shall we change direction?" Danny suggested. "It is absolutely rancid."

Luca shook his head. "No. Those things could smell us. If anything, this could mask our scent. I would hope! It is certainly strong enough."

The men ran on further into the forest until the vicious odour overcame them both. Danny heaved, bringing up his last meal while he held on to a birch for support. Luca covered his nose with his hand, resisting the urge to do the same. He could feel bile travelling up his throat but he swallowed down hard and took a sip of water from his flask.

Danny desperately tried to compose himself, breathing in the tree's bark while Luca scanned the terrain around them.

"I think I see smoke, coming from over there," Luca whispered, pointing through the trees. Danny looked up with one eye, trying not to move his head. "Come on, I know it is rotten but we need to move," Luca instructed. Danny sighed but followed him, covering the lower half of his face with his robe.

As they got closer to the smoke, they could see at ground level the sparks of a fire through the window of a tiny cottage. Relief washed over Danny and he lurched forward, desperate for the protection of the little house, but Luca held him back.

"Just wait," he implored. "We have no clue as to who might be inside. It could be worse than the harpies."

Danny scoffed at the suggestion but agreed to approach it slowly. Crouching down in the bushes that surrounded them, they watched the cottage for several minutes, able to see each room lit up against the darkness of the forest.

The cottage was all one floor, topped with a pitched, uneven roof where a small chimney sat haphazardly;

looking like it could tumble through the loose tiles at any moment. Two windows looked out to the front of the house; each one set either side of a black, wooden front door. The door itself was adorned in the upper centre with a wrought iron cat's head, holding a ring in its mouth which served as a door knocker. A thick layer of dusty cobwebs suggested it had not been used for some time. Though the two windows were tainted with a layer of black dirt, the men could see into the rooms clearly.

"The place is empty. I am quite sure no one is there," Danny concluded.

Luca punched his arm, "Fool. Who set the fire then, and the candles burning in each room?"

"Oh, yes," Danny agreed, rubbing his arm.

However, there were definitely no obvious signs of life. The men moved closer, crouching under the windows. They peered inside but still, nothing stirred. Luca held on to the rotting wooden window frame and stood up slightly, scanning the room before him. It was hard to tell if it was a bedroom, kitchen or bathroom, such was the chaotic state of the place. There were certainly bowls of what once was food on the table at the side of the room. At the opposite side was a heap of stained shawls and blankets that could serve as a bed. Next to that, was a metal bucket, pushed up against the wall. Luca dared not imagine its contents.

He felt a tap on his shoulder and turned his head, seeing Danny looking through another window, a good six feet away. He turned around quickly, his eyes opening in terror, and fell back into the wall of the house. Danny saw it too and recoiled in utter shock. They were not alone.

"Looking for me?" the creature asked, laughing maniacally. It darted between the men and had opened the cottage door, jumped inside and slammed the door behind it before the men could comprehend what they had seen, and more so, what they had smelt. Luca could suppress it no longer and he heaved loudly, vomiting into a bush.

"What the hell was that?" Danny cried.

Between dry heaves, Luca managed to reply.

"I could not swear to it, but I think we may have found Peabody!"

The king had not been wrong in his description. She truly was a vile creature. Only about three feet in height, her belly was completely round. She did not appear to have legs, just ankles and feet, rendering her movements a waddle rather than a walk. She had no hair atop her scalp but long, straggly strands around the base. The scalp itself was wrinkled and red, with crusty yellow patches of dried puss. A deep scar ran from her forehead down to her jaw, intersecting her left eye which operated completely independently from the other, like a giant lizard. The few teeth she had were yellowed and gnarled, and her large, purplish nose bent to the side with a bulbous knoll at the unnatural joint.

The sight of her had been quite the shock, but it was her stench that the men struggled to forget; burned into their nostrils as it was. They watched again through the window as the short figure took a posy of herbs and lit them on a candle. She darted around the room, wafting the burning leaves around like an orchestral conductor. She moved quickly despite her disfigured form.

Luca knocked loudly on the rotting wooden door.

"What are you doing?" Danny whispered.

Luca ignored him, knocking again and looking back through the window at the strange little woman. She had stopped her crazy dance and was waddling towards the door.

A hidden little window towards the top of the door opened suddenly.

"Yes?" a blunt voice chirped.

Now that she had answered, Luca wasn't sure what to say. He looked at Danny for ideas but the man just shrugged. The little window snapped shut and Danny watched her resume her bizarre ritual. Luca knocked again. The little window opened.

"Yes?" her little voice blurted again.

"Sorry to bother you," Luca began.

"Good. Do not do it again." The little window snapped shut.

"Oh, for goodness' sake," Danny muttered. He stepped up to the door, knocked loudly and did not bother to wait for the window to flap open. "My name is Sir Daniel and my comrade is Luca. We have been sent by King William of Thistlewick. He believes you may be able to assist us. You go by 'Peabody' do you not?"

The little window remained closed. They waited a moment.

Luca knocked again.

"Peabody," he said gently, "please. We need your help."

They both focussed on the tiny window. It remained shut, but instead, the main door slowly began to open. A stench more ferocious than their previous encounters, wafted out, attacking their senses. Both men covered their noses and mouths. Luca spoke through the cloth of his overcoat.

"Please may we come in? It is nightfall and we have already been too close to some flying harpies."

"They will not come here," the small woman declared.

"Please." Luca said again, gesturing for her to open the door further.

She looked suspiciously at them, clearly hesitant to let these strangers into her home, but she cautiously allowed them entrance. Luca had to duck down to get through the door. He looked back at Danny though and winked, tapping the top of the door frame, "You need not worry, flyspeck."

Chapter 11

Thyella reached Thistlewick quickly; such was her desire to taste human flesh once more. She flew promptly to the farmlands on the edge of the village, certain that some of her sisters would be tempted here in the hopes of finding unsheltered livestock. It happened rarely, though, so vigilant were the villagers in ensuring all animals were safely contained each night.

She had been right in her assumption. Two of her sisters stood motionless on the roof of a hay barn, scanning the land for signs of movement. She landed next to them and told them of her earlier encounter. As she passed on Typhonia's orders to find these men, she could see them salivating with keen anticipation. The assurance she gave them of hunting actual humans was met with absolute elation. The three of them worked together to seek out the others, advising them to discard the scraps of woodland vermin they had gathered, with promises of a far more lavish meal.

The women flew in unison with Thyella at the helm of the formation darting towards the dam. They had never flown so swiftly, relishing the thought of sinking their teeth into human flesh. As they neared the house on top of the dam, the smell of man was intoxicating. Though it soon became clear that the building was empty, they were not disappointed, knowing the men could not have gone far. The women worked in pairs, spreading out, to cover as many miles as possible in search of their precious prizes.

They weaved through the trees with expert precision, flaring their nostrils and sniffing the air to track the trail of human odour. Each time though, the task led them into the forest beyond the dam, and their senses became skewed. They lost their hearing, flying erratically in the sudden silence. Their vision became blurry and they could no longer track a living creature.

Infuriating hours passed without the slightest success. The scent had been lost and any signs of movement they perceived were just the same small animals they ate daily. Thyella's heart began to race as any hope of triumph disappeared with the lightened sky of a rapidly approaching morning. They had failed, and the consequences would be severe. Panicked, the women foraged for what they could, terrified of returning empty handed. There would be scolding enough without a completely fruitless night.

Chapter 12

Luca and Danny sat at the table in the depressing and pungent room. Danny was sure that the fabric of his chair was wet but he dared not feel it with his hands. The look of disgust on his face was obvious and Luca glared at him, willing politeness to appease their host.

The men looked around them, taking in their surroundings. Not one square inch of wall was spare, filled as they were with paintings, candles sat in ornate sconces, various animal skulls and bouquets of dried flowers hanging upside down. Each object was coated in thick layers of dust and strewn with cobwebs hanging between them like macabre, grey bunting.

The floor of the room could once have been stone, but was now so covered in dirt, soot and discarded, rotting vegetable peelings, it was difficult to tell. The only clean item in the entire room appeared to be a small, framed portrait on the mantel of the fireplace, depicting a young, pretty woman with dark hair tied neatly back, and striking dark eyes.

Next to the fireplace was built floor-to-ceiling oak shelving, packed with far more books than it was designed to contain. Each upright section of volumes served to hold several more, lying flat on top.

The round-bellied woman boiled a pan of brown-looking water on the stove. She selected two dusty tankards, blew into them, wiping the rims with her dirty hands and poured the liquid into the vessels, setting them down in front of each of her guests.

They thanked her, but neither drank.

"You are Peabody?" Danny asked again.

The woman stared at the floor. She looked almost ashamed.

"That is what they call me," she said. "You mentioned the king. If you are here, he must be near the end." The men nodded.

"You know, then, what he needs from you?" Luca asked.

"I know what he *wants* of me," she replied bitterly. "Do you not?"

The men looked at each other, hesitant to disclose their naivety to the details.

"Not exactly," Luca vaguely replied. "Will you do it, though?"

She wrinkled her deformed nose and looked at the men. "No!" She said bluntly and picked up, once again, the smouldering remains of the leaves, resuming her erratic dance. "You may stay the night, however. And when the sun rises, you can sod off from whence you came, though do give my regards to your king."

Danny looked livid. "The king assured Luca that you could help. That you could be trusted, and if we found you, we would be saved."

She laughed and looked at Luca. She asked what other falsehoods the king had told him. But Luca knew the king had not lied; that this woman would be their saviour. He could feel it in his bones. He stood up and walked over to her, placing his huge hands on her tiny shoulders.

"The king told me you were brilliant." She blushed suddenly and coyly averted her eyes. "He told me to trust you, and I think I can. And he told me you were wise, and deep down in your heart, I think you know that ending this will help you too."

Her eyes darted to meet Luca's gaze.

"I liked the man," she said. "But he did nothing for me or my family. His ancestors banished my kind. I will return that favour with apathy towards your cause." She toddled over to the pile of stained blankets and sheets, turning several times within the rotten bedding like a sleepy terrier, seeking rest and comfort.

Danny's face flashed with anger. He stepped towards her filthy sleeping spot, but Luca held him back and shook his head.

"We shall rest here and then leave you be, Peabody," he assured her. "Thank you for your hospitality though. It has been an eventful day."

Chapter 13

The wrath of Typhonia knew no bounds and even the cathedral's walls seemed to quake with her rage. She had longed for human flesh to quench her growing hunger but her ineffectual slaves had, once again, returned with morsels.

"It could not be helped," Thyella pleaded. "Their scent was lost in the old witch's territory. You know we cannot go there."

Typhonia strolled up to Thyella, her face inches from hers. Kykie skulked around the altar, fearing her leader's next move.

"They should not have had chance to shield under her ancient powers. You have failed!" she shouted. She threw Thyella against the hard, stone wall. The blonde harpy crumbled to the ground, whimpering. Typhonia had not finished. She hoisted Thyella up by her wings flinging her body into the air where she slammed into the altar.

"Stand, Thyella, stand," she ordered.

The injured woman shakily rose to her feet and looked at her queen in terror.

"Now, fly," Typhonia said, smiling and gesturing upwards.

Thyella looked up at the bell-tower, confused.

"It is daylight, my lady. I cannot."

"Oh, I beg to differ, my dear. You are more than able to. It will be your last flight but you certainly can."

The others shared frightened glances. A nervous uncertainty swept through their thoughts; surely their queen would not make their sister carry out such an act.

"My lady, please." Thyella begged. "I did everything I could. I saved Aeraki. I carried her all the way back here to safety. We tried to find the men but lost their scent. They must be away from the village for good purpose. They may be out again at nightfall. I can find them." But Typhonia would not be dissuaded.

"You have let them escape once. I will not be giving second chances again." Thyella's grey face was wet with tears, knowing she could not overpower her leader.

"Please," she pleaded again, sobbing. "Please, my lady."

Typhonia glided to Thyella's side. She stroked her blonde hair, and whispered into her ear.

"Fly."

Thyella looked to her sisters for help. Her creased face seeking out assistance from their watchful eyes. But each woman kept their eyes averted, too afraid to become embroiled in the anguished scene before them. Even Aeraki, who had been quite willing to contradict Typhonia on many occasions, remained quiet, although her wounds were still fresh and her strength not fully regained.

"You have but two choices, Thyella," Typhonia mused. "You can make the choice of self-sacrifice to redeem yourself of your mistakes, which would be an honourable death. Or, your sisters can watch as I force you into the open air with my own hands. It is of no consequence to me which option you choose. The outcome will be the same, but the second choice would be a cowardly and undignified demise. If that is how you wish to be remembered, by all means fight me, Thyella. You will lose, however, and I will ensure your death is preceded with agony."

Thyella crumbled to the floor as the blunt realisation overwhelmed her. There was no way out. She could not hope to defeat Typhonia; her individual strength far exceeded the collective of the others. She stood to her full height, tears streaming down her haunted face as she spread her wings one last time and shot into the sky.

A stunned silence spread through the room. Typhonia calmly returned to the altar, picking at the pathetic spoils once more. It had been a long time since she had destroyed one of her own and it had given her an appetite.

Chapter 14

Peabody was already awake when Luca and Danny began to stir. They had slept remarkably well on the floor of the stone cottage, wrapped in their overcoats and robes, the fire crackling peacefully in the grate and bringing gentle warmth to the room.

"Eat," Peabody ordered as she placed three bowls on the table. Luca and Danny sat up, sleepily and joined her in the dining area, tentatively looking at the meal before them. Danny scratched at his neck, the wounds from his vicious encounter, itching at his raw skin. Peabody ate like she hadn't in days, shovelling great spoons of the off-white, clotted looking substance into her mouth. Much of it dribbled down her chin but she didn't seem to notice. She belched loudly between mouthfuls, forcing Danny to excuse himself as he ran outside to be sick once more.

Luca over-compensated for his fellow traveller's weak stomach, taking a great spoonful of the mixture and shoving it quickly into his mouth. It was surprisingly sweet and could almost pass as pleasant.

Danny remained outside for several minutes and Luca tried to conceal the audible retching with appreciative noises for the barely palatable breakfast. He idly took the pocket watch from his breeches, flicked it open and glanced at the early hour, not really noting what time the hands revealed. As he snapped the casing shut, Danny returned to the room, looking terribly pale but taking his seat at the table with as casual a demeanour as he could muster.

Peabody's right eye stared at the little man, taking in his clammy skin and gaunt expression. Her left eye, moving quite on its own, spotted the shiny, golden object in Luca's hand as he moved to replace it in his pocket.

"What is that?" she asked. Luca, still gripping the item, pulled it back out of his breeches.

"My pocket watch," he shrugged. "I had just pondered the hour."

"May I see?" she asked. He handed her the watch and she turned it over in her dirty fingers, looking intently at the design etched in its surface. "It is very lovely," she declared. "From where did you acquire it?"

"It was found with Luca," Danny explained, "when he was just a baby."

"The king told me it would keep me safe," Luca laughed. "He may have been correct in that. Here I am, still alive and well."

Peabody snapped the watch shut, handed it back to Luca, and looked at the men.

"I will help with your quest," she suddenly declared. "It will be, as you say, beneficial to all. But first you must finish your breakfast. You will be no good to me hungry."

The men smiled at each other in surprise, relieved that they had secured their king's chosen ally.

"How are we to proceed today, then?" Danny asked. "The king believes that finding Luca's mother will reveal our path out of this hell."

Peabody finished eating and put down her spoon. She used the back of her hand to wipe away the remnants from around her mouth and then wiped that on the bizarre yellow sack she was wearing as a dress.

"Luca's mother?" Peabody asked, cynically. "No, no. There are far more pressing issues at hand. Four elements need putting in their place," she mused, almost to herself. "We shall start with the Water Spirits. They, at least, are easy to find. Where the rivers flow and greet the Earth, the Spirits dance at water's birth."

"If you think that is best," Luca agreed. "And how do we 'put them in their place'?"

"We ask them," she replied, simply. She looked at Luca strangely, taking in his face. "You are very handsome," she said suddenly.

"Thank you," he said, awkwardly.

Danny raised his eyebrows, still scratching at his neck, and Luca scowled at him. Peabody stood quickly and waddled towards the small man.

"Let me see," she said, moving his hand away from the gouges in his throat. "Itchy?" she asked. Danny nodded, trying to scratch again, but she pushed his hand away. "It will only make it worse," she warned. "Stay still."

She waddled over to the fireplace where a vast array of dusty bottles adorned the mantel piece, all differing in size and shape. After looking carefully at the aged, hand-written labels, she selected a glass flagon and carried it to the kitchen area. She poured a few drops of the clear liquid contents into a bowl, and threw in some chopped white pieces of what appeared to be some sort of vegetable. Using the back of a wooden spoon, she ground the contents into a paste and shuffled back to Danny. He was scratching again at his neck and she batted his hand away, giving him a stern look.

"It is best to treat a harpy's scratch the same way we would treat the harpy itself," she said. Danny looked at her confused. She leant closer and answered his quizzical expression. "Do not anger it!"

With her little fingers she carefully dabbed the mixture along the lines of his scratches, then smeared the remaining paste around his reddening skin.

Almost instantly Danny's desire to scratch had ceased. A soothing cool replaced the burning itch that had tormented him since the attack. He looked at the little lady gratefully and thanked her in earnest.

"Right, I need you to bring me a dead fish," she suddenly requested of him. "And Luca, I need you to bring me a live bird. Then we can begin our day."

It was several hours before the men returned. Securing a fish had been relatively easy. Danny had waded into the river, and then stood completely still and silent, for several minutes, hoping the waters would not turn against him and begin to rush into his precarious stance. Thankfully they remained calm, and schools of fish were soon teeming around his ankles. With speed and precision, he forced his sword into the water and straight through the scaly flesh of a writhing trout.

Capturing a live bird, however, had not been quite so simple. Luca had climbed into the branches of a tree, his robe outstretched in his hands. There were plenty of birds flying around and an equal number darting across the forest floor in search of food. Luca had waited until a bird was positioned under him and then let his robe float down to enclose the creature. The time taken for the robe to reach the ground, however, gave ample opportunity for each of the chosen birds to scarper. Luca climbed back out of the tree and searched the ground for small but weighty pebbles. Having found four good contenders, he tied them into the edges of his robe and took his position back in the tree. With the additional weight, the robe fell quickly, when another bird landed nearby. There were several further failed attempts, but with one last effort, Luca spied a blackbird pulling at a worm from under a grassy mound. He carefully dropped his robe and the grown men actually cheered with joy as the cloth covered the bird. Luca delicately folded the robe around the immobile blackbird and they returned to Peabody's cottage.

She was waiting for them and opened the door before they had even had chance to knock. She clapped her hands in glee as she saw they had been successful in their feats. Before the men could step into the cottage, Peabody had donned a robe and headscarf, and marched out, gesturing for them to follow. They were clearly heading back to the river and Danny wondered why she hadn't just met them there.

The half-mile walk took far longer with the tiny woman in tow. They reached a clearing and Peabody ordered Danny and Luca to stay out of sight. She took the dead fish from Danny's hand and pocketed it in her robe. Then she gently unfolded the layers of cloth in Luca's outstretched arms and softly cradled the blackbird in her hands.

"This will not take long," she assured them as she waddled towards the bank of the calmly-flowing river. Danny leant against a tree and Luca used his robe to sit down on the mulched leaves and twigs of the forest floor.

"Do you have any idea what this will entail?" Danny asked. Luca shook his head. "Do you have any idea how appalling she will smell now there is a dead fish in her clothes?" Danny pondered. Luca would have shot him a look but it was a fair point.

Peabody was at the river's edge. She held the little bird up to her face, speaking gently to the animal in a low, calming voice. She looked around her as if performing to an audience and then held the little bird up into the air above her head. Without a minute's hesitation she swiftly snapped its neck.

The men looked on, shocked. They had each been unsure of what to expect but it had not been that. They watched as Peabody bent down and scooped up great handfuls of wet earth from the bank, creating a deep hole. She placed the bird's body into the hollow and then returned the earth, covering the bird and patting down the sandy soil. She still appeared to be talking to something as she took the dead fish out of her robes and popped it into the water. As it floated on top of the ebbing current, a glow of golden light began to appear around it, spreading out across the river. Luca stood up to see clearly and he and Danny watched in amazement as the fish began to move, wriggling around before disappearing under the surface, alive once more. Peabody turned to her left and bowed, then turned to face the river, bowing again, and once more to her right. She then turned her back on the waters and began her slow ascent away from the bank, to Danny and Luca.

Without a word she walked between them, heading in the direction of her home. When they didn't follow, she turned around and looked at their awe-struck faces.

"Come on then," she called out. "We have not got all day." After bearing witness to that magical display, they did not need telling twice.

When the unlikely trio reached Peabody's cottage, Danny braced himself for the toxic odour, but entering the little house, the men were pleasantly surprised. The main room no longer housed the stinking bedding, vile bucket and mouldy surfaces, but was a clean and tidy kitchen and sitting room. Through a little door they could see three made-up beds and there were even vases of fresh flowers placed around the cosy abode. Peabody looked at their surprised expressions.

"I was not prepared for guests last night," she said simply. It was only now the men noticed that Peabody herself had changed into clean clothes and appeared to have washed.

"It looks lovely, Peabody," Luca said, kindly. Peabody smiled, her teeth appearing whiter than before.

"The Water Spirits are assuaged for now," she said. "They will bother you no more."

"Excellent," Danny said. "That seemed fairly undemanding. One down, three to go: the Earth, the Fire Spirits, and of course, the Daughters of the Wind. What do you have planned for those, my friend?"

Peabody's little face glowed.

"*Friend*," she repeated. "Well, I am afraid we have not quite finished with the Water Spirits. We still need to free them," Peabody said, as if it was obvious. "Destroy the dam and the Water Spirits will be released. We will need their help later, as well as the stones of the structure. They are appeased for now and will cause no more chaos, but this will truly bring them happiness. That is rare for Water Spirits; usually they are evil, miserable blighters."

Luca smiled. He was beginning to like the strange little lady. "*Miserable blighters!*" he laughed.

Peabody's eyes met his suddenly. "Oh, it is nothing to laugh at. Their misery knows no bounds and they use it to feed on our fears. Not only can they decide, all of a sudden, to rush faster if they feel a human presence, they can make you wish to enter the water, quite against your will, to begin with."

Luca and Danny looked at each other in shock.

"What do you mean by that?" Luca asked, suddenly appearing angry. "What do they do?"

Peabody stood back, uncertain why the mood had changed so quickly. "Well, they make you see things," she explained. "Things that should not be in the water. Many excitable fishermen have lost their lives at the sudden appearance of gold beneath the current. Greed at its worst, I fear — there is no gold in the Thistlewick River. I heard once of a little boy diving into the water, certain he had seen his beloved dog in the choppy current. Fortunately, he was rescued and reminded that his dog had passed away several weeks earlier."

Tears glistened in Luca's eyes as he listened to her.

"What about a child?" he asked, his lips trembling. "Have you heard of someone seeing a child?"

Peabody nodded gently. "Ah, yes. That is, of course, the cruellest of illusions. Few observers of that deceitful apparition would stand idly by on the safety of the land. As I said, they are miserable little blighters."

Luca sat down on a small wooden dining chair, unable to stay on his feet, as the truth behind his beloved Nancy's drowning became clear in his grieving mind. Florence must have seen a child after all. Though a fictitious vision created by the river, it would have appeared real enough to her. He stared at the freshly swept stone floor of the cottage, in a sorrowful silence.

Danny looked at Peabody's confused expression but did not feel an explanation would be appropriate in Luca's dismay. He thought back to the task in hand and how they could ensure the tragedy would never be repeated.

"How do we destroy the dam, Peabody?" Danny asked with new determination. "It is, after all, enormous and appears to be of solid structure."

Peabody suddenly ran from the room and returned almost instantly carrying a sledgehammer twice her height, with a look on her face of pure delight.

"This will do," she said.

Danny eyed the object. "It really will not," he said, shaking his head and looking at Peabody as though she was completely crazy.

"Danny!" Luca scolded. He stood up, having roused himself from his dark thoughts, and walked over to Peabody. He gently took the sledgehammer from her hands and held it up. "Sweetheart, this is not going to impact that huge dam. It would barely chip a corner of any of the stones."

"*Sweetheart*," she repeated, to herself, looking at her tall guest with tears twinkling in her eyes. She smiled up at him and pointed to the sledgehammer. "This will do," she said again. "Trust me."

The words of the king resonated in Luca's mind and he cursed himself for doubting her, particularly after the events they had just observed. Still holding the tool, he nodded.

"Of course we trust you, Peabody. We really do and truly appreciate all that you are doing." He looked at Danny. "Do we not?!"

"Absolutely," Danny agreed, ashamed at himself for mocking their new ally. He looked once more at the sledgehammer. "So, is this magical?" he enquired, sincerely. "One hit, and the dam explodes?"

"Of course not," she laughed, looking at him like he was the crazy one. "It is but a sledgehammer!" She trotted once again out of the house. Luca followed, carrying the hammer. As he passed Danny he laughed and muttered,

"*Is it magical*? My word! How did you receive a knighthood?"

Chapter 15

Getting sick and tired of trudging back and forth to the river, Danny lagged behind, leaving Luca to stroll next to Peabody as she walked as quickly as she could with her strange gait.

"Have you ever been to Thistlewick, Peabody?" Luca asked, making small talk to break the silence.

"My kind would not be welcomed there."

"But you do know the king?" he asked.

"He came to see me once, yes. Nice man."

"What did he say to you?" he pressed.

"Many things," she answered. "He stayed for several hours."

Luca understood she did not want to share. He stopped pressing and continued in silence. All of a sudden Peabody stopped walking, her head down. She turned to Luca.

"He asked me about my mother. She had been, after all, the cause of the childless state of Thistlewick. And he asked me about my great-grandmother's sister, many times removed, who had cursed the village through her rage and raised the elements from their peaceful equilibrium. And he asked how I made my tea. He liked it." She turned back and carried on walking.

"Wait. What?" Luca said, stunned. "You are the daughter of Greta?"

"Yes. That was her name." Peabody mused, continuing her arduous hike.

"Goodness," Luca pondered. "Did the king not just request that you lift the curses?"

"My mother's curse had already faded with her death. When the king befriended me there were already children, once more, in Thistlewick. And as for that of my ancestor, that is the task we now undertake. If truth be told, I knew little of her, but the legends. Her time here was many generations ago, and though tales have been passed down through the ages, these events alter with each telling. Recollections vary with time. I did know that lifting her particular essence of dark magic, could not be done earlier, however. It had to be the right time."

"Why is that?" he asked.

"Ah, you will see. Our timing is dictated to us by a much greater force than a witch's magic, on this occasion. All will become clear. I will say this for your king; he is a kind and very wise man."

Luca nodded. "Yes. I am beginning to appreciate that now. Have you ever heard of a woman called Phoebe?" Luca asked, remembering the note the king had found in his watch.

"Phoebe?!" she pondered. She looked at Luca. "No. I have never heard of a woman called Phoebe."

Luca was disappointed. He had spent his life believing he would never know his origins, and he had found peace with that fact. He had, after all, been raised by a lovely woman and had as good a childhood as possible under the cloud of Thistlewick. The discovery of the pocket watch note however, had given him renewed ambition to seek the story of his background. It seemed, though, that the king may have been mistaken in believing this journey would begin with Luca's parentage. He certainly seemed to have been right about Peabody, though. She appeared more than capable in her own strange little ways.

"Right, we are here!" Peabody exclaimed.

They waited for Danny to reach them as Peabody jumped from boulder to giant boulder at the edge of the forest.

"Good, good," she kept muttering to herself. "Yes, yes, very good. They will like these."

"Why have we stopped?" Danny asked. "The dam is right over there." It was at least another two hundred feet to the weir.

"Because this is where the rocks are, Sir Daniel!" she said, pointing around her. She took the huge hammer from Luca's hands, feeling its weight. Handing it back to him she gestured to the boulders.

"Do you need me to break them up?" he asked.

"Of course," she replied. "They will not fit like that."

Luca didn't question her. He wanted her to know that he trusted her bizarre requests, although he did wonder to himself quite how this was helping. Lifting the heavy sledgehammer up over his shoulder, he slammed it down onto the edge of one of the huge stones. A slight crack appeared down the middle and he smashed it again, this time breaking it into four jagged parts.

Peabody smiled and pointed to the next target. He continued the process over and over, until at least thirty boulders had been broken into pieces, while the tiny woman nodded her approval.

"Right, Sir Daniel, you can start with these ones," she said, pointing to some of the larger pieces. Danny furrowed his brow, confused. "We need to carry them to the water's edge," she explained. "They will not be able to reach them from here, will they?" she laughed. "Half must go behind this side of the dam, and half must go in front. That is very important."

Danny, too, chose not to question her, and he and Luca began the long and gruelling task of carrying the broken rocks to the water's edge. Hours of labour went into the undertaking, the pile of rubble gradually appearing smaller with each journey. Their hands were blistered, arms and legs ached, but eventually each piece had been transported in turn, and now rested on the bank.

"Excellent!" Peabody cried, clapping her hands together in excitement. "And now, we must wait."

The exhausted men leant against trees to rest their aching limbs. They watched in anticipation at the river's periphery, not knowing what exactly they were waiting for. Luca looked around him, conscious of the ever-darkening skies over head.

"Do not fear," Peabody whispered, "it will not take them long, once they have commenced."

After a few moments more, Luca thought he saw some movement, one of the boulders in front of the weir, edging further into the water. Then another one, without a doubt, slid from the bank to the lapping, murky water. In turn each jagged stone disappeared from view, sinking beneath the current.

Peabody squealed with delight.

"Those water spirits are truly amazing when they are feeling agreeable. They have done a marvellous job, have they not?" She asked. "Now I do believe it is time for tea, gentlemen." She turned her back to the river and toddled away, followed by a bemused Luca and Danny.

"They?" Danny muttered to Luca, looking most unappreciated. "Did she not see our efforts? I do believe that we did a *marvellous job*."

Luca couldn't help but laugh. "Oh, Danny, I saw your hard work, do not fret."

Chapter 16

Meredith sat in the high-backed chair next to King William's four-poster bed. Alone with him as his servants slept, she watched closely as the old man struggled on. Beads of sweat tumbled down his temple, although his body shivered with the cold. He no longer had the energy or inclination to sit at the fire, even with company present. He had known the kind lady for many years, though, and thought she would forgive him the informality. With the exception of Luca, he was, after all, the only man she had ever truly loved.

His chest expanded and collapsed with rattling effort; each breath desperate. He could feel every erratic heartbeat as his body fought against death. He looked at Meredith, still beautiful in her winter years and remembered fondly the sparkle in her eyes when they were together in her youth. He was far older than her, but he would happily have married her, had her father not forbidden the union. It was not the king's age that had disturbed the fearful man, but the family's damned embroilment in the witch's curse.

"Two more days, Your Majesty. Just two more days," Meredith encouraged, quietly. She gently brushed away a curl of grey hair from his forehead and held his trembling hand. "Then you can go in peace."

He smiled at her and gripped her fingers with his. As he gazed into her eyes, he regretted each hour he had not been by her side. Each year he had spent pretending to love another instead of fighting for the one who held his heart. He knew she could read his thoughts as she stroked his hand.

"You saved my life, William. You need to know that. You saved my life the day you brought Luca to me. I had wanted to live for you but my father's cruel decision had left me with nothing. I know he had meant well but I had longed for death. You gave me someone else to live for though." She wiped the tears from her cheeks as the gratitude she felt overwhelmed her. "I will always love you William, and for giving me Luca, even more so."

Her confession brought tears to the king's eyes and they cried together for the life they had longed for together, but that never was.

A harsh coughing fit erupted from the king and his imminent death was once more brought to the forefront of his thoughts. He opened a small drawer in his nightstand, took out a scroll, tied neatly with a red ribbon, and handed it to Meredith.

"You must reveal this to the council, when I am gone," he said. "It has taken many years for me to piece this together. I could not leave my village without a suitable sovereign."

Meredith looked puzzled. She knew there was no such heir.

"It is a misconception that King Frederick's family were killed in the revolt," the king explained, seeing her bemused expression. "His children survived and there is a living descendent. It is a stroke of good fortune for the village. A rare occurrence, I know, but there we have it, and I am certain they are of good character and will rise to the occasion admirably."

Meredith tucked the scroll into her bag, smiling at the king's determination to leave no stone unturned. She would read it when the time came.

"Has word been sent to her?" he whispered. His face creased with pain each time he spoke.

"She is aware," Meredith nodded, reassuringly, "and she is ready."

Chapter 17

After gorging on a hefty meal of stew, bread and cheese, Luca, Danny and Peabody sat, warming themselves at the little fireplace.

"That was a beautiful dinner, Peabody. Thank you." Luca said, rubbing idly at his blistered hands. Danny nodded his agreement and patted his very full stomach. They had needed a good meal after their busy day.

"Forgive me, though, Peabody. I am a little confused," Danny ventured. "I had thought we needed to destroy the dam to free the Water Spirits. How have we done that?"

"Oh, we have not," Peabody said, bluntly. "What we have done is given the spirits all the tools they need to destroy it themselves."

None-the-wiser Danny asked how.

"Well, you see, the dam was built to suppress the continual flooding of Thistlewick, riled as the spirits were by Magissa's spell. But it always had to allow a small flow. The village could not be without a source of water for one thing, but also because the strength of a completely hampered current would build and build. No wall, no matter how sturdy, could hold it forever.

"Now, though, as we rest, some of the spritely, little spirits will be pushing the rocks we placed in front of the dam, down-stream to Thistlewick. They will carefully press the boulders up against the river bank closest to the village to ensure there is sufficient barrier in place to protect against the work of their friends further up the river. Their little weir-workmates will be toiling away, using the rocks we placed behind the dam to plug the gaps left deep down on the river bed. The pressure will build quickly, the spirits will push with all their might, and the walls of the dam will crack and crumble, freeing our new friends." She paused. "I apologise, Sir Daniel, I thought that was obvious. Now, please excuse me gentlemen, I must retire."

She got to her feet, heading towards the newly made bedroom, but Luca stopped her. He leant down and kissed her scarred forehead.

"You really are a little, magical genius!" he declared. A girly giggle escaped her and she slipped off to slumber.

It did not take long before the two men could hear a rapturous snoring coming from the bedroom. Danny laughed.

"Bless her," he said. "She is a strange little marvel. Of that, I am certain."

Luca smiled. "She really is. When I spoke to her today, she told me she is the daughter of Greta. That will be the source of her magic, I do not doubt."

Danny looked surprised. He had not given too much thought to her family tree, imagining she had been grown in a cauldron somewhere. Now though, the female line of her ancestry explained many of the sights they had witnessed over the past few days.

"Did she mention her father?" he asked. Luca shook his head and then an awful thought occurred to him.

"My word, do you think, the men Typhonia sent?"

"Oh, dear lord!" Danny said. "Let us hope not. That is a frightful thought."

A silence fell between them as they each pieced together the awful events that must have led to the birth of their new, odd associate. Danny rose and walked closer to the fireplace. Amongst the vases and bottles of lotions and potions, was a small framed portrait of a very beautiful young lady.

"Do you think this is her mother?" he asked, handing the picture to Luca. Luca looked at it carefully and nodded. "Do you think we can trust her entirely, Luca? After all, she is a witch's daughter, and her mother cast a terrible spell over Thistlewick."

"The king thought so," Luca replied. "You cannot deny she worked tremendous magic today, with the outcome we sought. I believe we can trust her. She has done nothing to suggest otherwise."

"I just find it bothersome now, knowing she is linked by blood to the two women who have caused these atrocities," Danny thought out loud.

"It is unfair to judge her based on family-members past. She is her own person and she seems kind of heart."

Danny nodded but did not look entirely convinced.

A clear night sky afforded Aeraki the rare luxury of favourable hunting conditions. She soared high above the canopy of forest oaks and birches, determined to seek out her prey. A seething anger burned inside of her. She had lost Thyella and felt an unfamiliar sorrow at the memory of her death. She had hated Typhonia for many centuries, but now her rage was growing. If only she had been strong enough to offer some defence to her sister, but their queen was well aware that she was at her weakest following the attack.

Ashamed that she had allowed herself to succumb to injury, the fury she felt over the loss of her arm, could only be soothed through revenge. She would find the discourteous men and she would make them her next meal. And she vowed to herself, she would not be sharing their precious flesh with her leader.

Closely escorted by two of her sisters, she followed the river, against its flow. They soared through the air, hoping to catch the scent again near the dam, and take their time this night in tracking where it led. Humans, on foot, could not outrun them forever.

They rounded the river's bend and looked forth towards the weir. But where the immense structure had once overlooked the landscape, were now just ruins, the river running freely between the remnants of the broken stones. Aeraki could see clearly that the water, though unhindered, was flowing calmly along its path.

She knew instantly the implications of the sight before her.

"The Water Spirits have been pacified," she howled in disbelief. "Weak!" she spat at the river. Suddenly, seeking out her prey seemed a trivial notion. They needed to inform Typhonia that the counter-curse had begun.

*"Go to sleep, Baby Joe,
No more tears must flow.
Time to rest, Baby Joe,
To Dreamland you must go."*

Luca woke early, a lovely melody, as always, churning in his mind. Danny was curled up under the covers of the adjacent bed, just a foot sticking out over the edge of the frame. He could see nothing of Peabody, just a mound of bedding, but he could certainly hear her; the rattling snores echoing off the walls.

Pottering around the kitchen, he managed to put together a breakfast of porridge, eggs, bread and cheese, ready for his sleeping companions to wake and face another day. As they gratefully ate their food and drank their hot tea, Danny asked Peabody what tasks lay ahead of them.

"Of the Earth, for the Earth, today we shall build," she replied. Danny sighed. He had been hoping for a less physical task.

They made a small clearing on the forest floor and Peabody lit five black candles in a circle and used small twigs to create a star, joining the candles at each of the points. She placed a large posy of sage, lavender and rosemary in the centre. Danny stared at the shape she had made on the ground, feeling uneasy at the image before him.

"Is that not a pentagram, Peabody?" he asked.

"It is," she replied curtly.

"Is that not a sign of evil?" he questioned.

Peabody laughed. "That is quite a common misconception, Sir Daniel. The pentagram is a peaceful symbol though, in its essence. The five points represent the five elements, you see: Earth, Air, Fire, and Water are represented by the four lower points. Then, not to be forgotten is Spirit, sitting at the top point and overseeing nature." She followed the points of the star with her hand as she listed each facet, then stood and looked at Danny. She smiled reassuringly. "It is not in the least bit evil, believe me. I would never practice dark magic. I have seen the results of that work and would not wish to repeat it."

Still smiling at the men, she took a small black book from her purple velvet bag and thumbed through the pages, searching for a particular passage. Her fingers rested on a page and she read the words silently, memorizing each section. The men watched as she closed her eyes and began to perform a bizarre little dance around the area, reciting the Latin incantation under her breath, which neither Luca nor Danny understood. Peabody then instructed the men to dig a trench surrounding the layout of the candles, chopping through thick tree roots with an old axe to ensure a clear channel.

Peabody had given Danny a steel spade with a slightly rotting and split wooden handle, but he used it as best he could, pushing down on its blade with the heel of his foot. He heaved great mounds of peaty soil out of the trench, throwing them over his shoulder to a growing mound of earthly spoils. He struck the ground once more with the curved spade and pushed his foot against it, but this time it did not yield to his weight and he felt a crunching scrape beneath the blade.

"What is it?" Luca asked, seeing Danny stop his progress. Danny looked at Luca and tried again to force the spade into the ground but it would not go further.

"Something is underground," he said. "Not a tree root. At least, I think not." Luca put down the axe and walked to where Danny was stood. He took the spade from him and used it to scrape back the earth from the concealed object. Peabody had ceased her strange little dance and joined the men in studying the obstacle beneath the ground. Luca continued scraping at the soil until the three could clearly see that their grim discovery was an adult's skull.

They fell silent. Danny looked horrified but Luca, looking at the darkened bone, did not believe it was a recent burial. Peabody put her hands on her sides and sighed.

"What a very inconsiderate place to put a skull!" she said, with no apparent concern for its origins. She looked at the men quite perturbed that they did not seem to share her irritation. "Well, we will need to move it, now. That will take time."

She took the spade from Luca and began herself to scrape soil from around the skull until shoulders and the beginnings of a rib cage emerged. "It gets worse," she huffed. "I do believe it is a full body."

"Here, let me." Luca offered, taking the spade from the tiny lady and ploughing it into the ground next to skeletal remains. It did not take him long to clear the ground enough to see the bones of arms, hands, legs and feet. The body did not appear to have been buried with care; such was the way the limbs were strewn disorderly. Their owner had clearly been thrown in to the shallow grave, landing on their side and then packed down into the cavity with indifferent haste. As Luca scraped away the ground from the back of the body, he was surprised to see several additional bones jutting out from the rear of the rib cage and shoulder blades. He lurched back suddenly as he realised what they had unearthed. The skeleton had wings.

"Dear Lord!" Danny cried. "This is a harpy."

"Oh my!" Peabody said in a hasty turn of attitude. "The legend must be true, after all." The men looked at her, waiting for her to enlighten them but she continued to stare at the gruesome remains. Luca tried to determine if she was still perplexed at the delay in their work, or in the realisation of what she saw before her. She stood silently for many minutes taking in the details of the creature's remnants.

"What legend?" Danny asked abruptly, unable to wait any longer for an explanation.

"Ah, you would not know." Peabody realised. She sat down on the grave's edge and rested her feet on the harpy's ribcage; a move Danny cringed at. It seemed crudely unsympathetic, even to a creature such as this.

"I had always believed this was just a fable told through the generations," Peabody mused, "but this discovery, before us, suggests these whispers sometimes have their origin in truth." The men sat down on the forest floor, ready to listen to the tale, though neither ventured quite as close to the graveside as their little friend.

"I was always told that the creation of the harpies had not been Magissa's intention." Peabody began. "She was pleasantly surprised by her own powers at first. They had certainly served her needs perfectly in securing the throne for her son. He was crowned as an infant and Magissa was effectively queen until he came of age. Her first task, of course, was performing a counter-curse to the horrors she had unleashed upon Thistlewick. She performed her incantations to still the waters, calm the earth, halt the fires, and contrary to most rumours, banish the humanly forms of the wind back into the natural rush of wind.

"The harpies have always had a leader, but when first formed, that leader was not Typhonia. It was a harpy called Kataigida who had overseen their chaos and disruption under the dark magic of Magissa's curse. Kataigida, however, had strangely yielded quite happily to the counter-magic. She was preparing her colony to fly to the wind under the witch's new spell, and merge with the breeze once more.

"Sadly, unbeknown to her, two of her clan were not at all willing to placidly disappear and they persuaded the others to join them in their betrayal. Typhonia and Aeraki led the winged women to Kataigida's sleeping form and each of the harpies tore at her flesh with their teeth and talons, until they were certain she would no longer pose a threat to their unnatural lives. Typhonia and Aeraki were free to rule the harpies, flying by day and night to continue their torment of Thistlewick.

"Magissa was left hopeless, unable to undo her own curse and living in a constant fear that the villagers would, once again, revolt against the crown. She ordered the king's men to build a vast wall surrounding the manor house for additional protection. She knew however, the matter needed a more permanent solution. It soon occurred to her that the flying creatures had no honour, nor loyalty to each other, given their history of treachery. Magissa began to use this to her advantage. Typhonia and Aeraki shared power of the colony, but it was far from an amicable partnership and they often disagreed. Neither of the leaders though showed any willingness to step down. Aeraki was stubborn in her nature and Typhonia craved supremacy above all.

Eventually Magissa was left with little choice but to make a difficult decision to protect her son's reign. She bestowed upon Typhonia more strength and intelligence than the harpy had ever known. However, she could only exercise this strength if the harpies remained away from Thistlewick during daylight. At night, they were free to roam the skies wherever they pleased. Typhonia begrudgingly accepted, to secure power over Aeraki. As such, a dreadful but mutually beneficial treaty was formed. Magissa ensured Typhonia kept her word by casting a new spell; one that would cause the creatures to perish in sunlight.

"And this, I believe," Peabody concluded, pointing at the skeleton, "is the body of Kataigida. I do not know how this became her final resting place, though. It is most inconvenient."

"Crikey," Danny exclaimed.

"Indeed," Peabody agreed. "Now, what to do with it?" she pondered to herself, tapping her foot on the ribcage as the men looked away in disbelief.

Danny and Luca glanced at each other, wondering where their little helper had gained her indifferent response towards such things.

"I think we will re-bury her. Properly, though, this time," she suddenly declared. "She can rest in the centre of our gift to the earth. She did spout from nature somewhere down the line, after all."

Luca and Danny dug a large grave in the centre of their circle of candles. They gathered the bones of Kataigida, trying as best they could to keep them in order. They carefully placed her form into the grave, ensuring that each limb lay in its rightful place before re-filling the void with their mound of soil. Peabody replaced the twigs of her five-pointed star and stood back to admire the shrine.

Using the now discarded and broken stones of the old dam, and using wet soil and mud as rudimentary mortar, the men built a circular wall, carefully following Peabody's instructions.

When the final stone had been laid, they stood back and admired their work while rubbing their increasingly blistered hands.

"Good, good," Peabody muttered. "Yes, good. This will be appreciated."

She waddled over to Luca, standing as close as she could. She barely came up to his waist and the mountain of a man looked back down at her.

"And now, we must give the Earth another gift," she said. "Your watch, please, Luca," she ordered rather than asked.

"My pocket watch?" he asked. "But that is all I have from my... my past."

She placed her hand on his.

"And now, it will help to secure your future."

There was a pause but Luca finally conceded. He reached into his overcoat, pulled out the golden pocket watch and placed it delicately in Peabody's grasp.

"Thank you," she said sincerely, "and do not forget; your watch is not all you have from your past. You will still have the note."

She shuffled back to the circular wall, pulled herself up onto the top stone and disappeared within the make-shift walls, emerging moments later watch-less but with soil-encrusted fingers.

"There will be no more trembling grounds," she proclaimed.

With another day ended, another spell performed and another element appeased, they began their journey home to the cosy cottage. As they walked in a tired silence, Luca tried to remember when he had mentioned to the little sorceress, the note the king had found in his golden pocket watch.

Chapter 18

News of the happy Water-Fae did not displease Typhonia. It meant the journey had begun and King William had sent his chosen one on the perilous quest. This news vindicated her suspicions that the king's time was nearing an end. The unfortunate soul attempting to end Magissa's powerful curse may have had success with the spirits of the river, but they would never defeat the Daughters of the Wind. No, this was a good sign. Soon the king's heart would beat its final time, the treaty would end and they would fear the Sun no longer.

"What of the fires?" Typhonia asked. "Do they still burn?"

Aeraki nodded.

"There were several burning tonight." She confirmed.

Typhonia glided through the centre of the nave and stepped into the pit. She lay down on her front and placed her cheek against the cold, hard floor.

"The tremors have desisted. The Earth is at ease. He moves quickly, this chosen one... and he is not working alone!"

Her deep ebony eyes focussed on Kykie. With a motion as sudden as it was ferocious, she held Kykie by her neck, pushing her roughly against a stone pillar.

"He is working with *her!*" Typhonia snarled at the terrified harpy. "*She* would not be an obstacle if it were not for you!"

"Please," Kykie cried in desperation. "It cannot be. She could not possibly have lived long after that day."

Typhonia lifted Kykie clean into the air, launching her body into the pulpit where she crashed down hard; her head bouncing off the corner of the stone. She whimpered, trying to raise herself while the others watched on, most not daring to interject. Aeraki did not care enough to try.

"I think she did," Typhonia declared. "I think she has survived all this time, her powers growing. She is why our senses fail us in the forest beyond the dam. *She* is the reason we lose our vision there. That little witch." Her mind was reeling. She fumed at the realisation and suddenly regretted sparing Kykie all those years ago.

"She will stand in our way now," Typhonia yelled. "She will have mastered her mother's powers enough to defeat us."

"You defeated her mother though, my lady. Her daughter will be no match," Kykie reminded her.

"That is true," Typhonia mused. "*I* defeated her alone. And where were you, my dear? Betraying me, that is where."

The others were unsure of these revelations. They had not witnessed Typhonia's attack on Kykie long ago. Her wing had been savagely torn from her body, but no one spoke of it. Not one of them knew what had led to such a violent act. Typhonia saw the expressions on their faces.

"Ah, my lovelies, I have never disclosed to you your sister's defiance, have I? Well, allow me to elaborate." She glided to the altar and sat on its edge like an aged scholar, lecturing to keen and admiring young followers.

"You know of Greta, of course and how she failed us. We just needed her to use her craft to kill the king. But she was weak. The eager hunters that I had encouraged to seek out the lovely lady in the woods, should have finished her. Or, at the very least, ensured her existence was one of misery in their merriment.

"Sadly, one had morals," she spat, "and could no longer stand to see the treatment of the sorry wench at the hands of his fellows. He shot each one of them in turn.

"The witch had been harnessed and caged to suppress her powers, but he freed her, and went to make leave. Greta, though, grateful for his heroic act, thanked him and asked him to stay. Soon a love grew between them.

"Greta was with child and it was not his, but they raised her together, and after several years, another baby came along; this time, a boy. When I heard of this lovely life that *failure* had made for herself, I was understandably outraged.

"While you ladies were hunting, I went to pay her a little visit. Killing Greta and her lover was surprisingly easy, but her sneaky little daughter took the baby and ran. She had cast a blinding spell but it only gave her time enough to hide her brother, or so I thought." She glanced at Kykie, sneering.

"The brazen young lady returned and I was impressed enough to consider sparing her life. I merely broke her legs and twisted her spine, rendering her a squat little thing. I ripped her scalp clean off and very nearly blinded her, but I needed her to tell me where she had hidden the baby. She looked at me and said that she would rather die than tell me. In her pitiful state I thought that death would be a welcomed relief. So I left her alive to rot.

"I knew she could not have taken the child far, and I set off on foot, at first. But a movement in the trees alerted me to the presence of your sister, Kykie. There she was, babe in arms and I was delighted that she had found him. I soon realised, though, she was not there to assist me — she was saving the little thing.

"Kykie had always had the fastest flight and she never did reveal where she had left the child. But she never flew again.

"Now, that young lady has survived and she is helping our enemies. The daughter of Greta lives on. That witch's dirty, little offspring survives and her name is Phoebe."

Chapter 19

Luca and Danny had slept soundly following their day of hard labour, despite the relentless outpouring of snores erupting from Peabody's bed. Sitting down for a breakfast of porridge and tea, Danny was relieved that the offerings of food improved daily.

"Are we to placate the Fire Spirits today, Peabody?" he asked.

"No, no, we must not do that!" she replied. "We need them to remain irritated." She sipped on her tea, elaborating no further.

"The Wind, then?" he asked, afraid of the answer. "Are we to face those flying demons?"

Luca looked at Danny. He could see the terror in his eyes. Luca, though, was not afraid. He was more than willing to bring them to extinction.

"It has to be today," Peabody confirmed. "We will not get this opportunity again. Not while we three breathe." She finished her tea and stood up from the table. "We have a long walk ahead of us today, gentlemen. Let us delay no longer."

As they made their way out of the tiny cottage, Luca glanced into the bedroom, ensuring he had left behind nothing he would need. He looked twice and then a third time, astonished to see the room was empty. All three beds had disappeared. A wave of sadness seeped over him as he realised this meant it would be their final day together. The task was ending and they would be going home.

Peabody was waiting in the doorway for him, watching him staring into the little room that the three of them had shared. Luca looked at her and smiled,

"You could have left one bed for yourself, Peabody. It is surely an improvement to sleeping on your floor?" She shrugged her shoulders and smiled back, fondly.

Outside of the cottage was a warm and pleasant breeze. The sky was blue and not a cloud could be seen. Spring was coming to an end and making way for a beautiful summer.

"Lead the way, my lady," Danny said, gesturing to Peabody to go ahead.

"*My lady*," Peabody repeated to herself, her face colouring. She pointed up at the mountain that shadowed her cottage. "This way, gentlemen. Today we climb."

The tiny lady began her strange waddle towards the foot of the giant hill, a peculiar odour emanating from the purple, velvet shoulder bag she carried with her.

"The smell is back!" Danny whispered to Luca, flaring his nostrils.

Luca nodded. "At least we are outside," he whispered back. "Just stay down-wind."

Ascending the mountain was an immense task but Luca was impressed by the speed at which Peabody took each rocky step. As they climbed higher and higher, the breeze grew stronger, whipping at the trio with increasing ferocity. Luca heard the sound of gushing water getting louder and louder. He knew they were moving away from the river and wondered why its water's flow was echoing around him.

Danny, a few steps ahead of Luca, stopped suddenly and looked back.

"Did you feel that?" he asked. "The ground was shaking."

Luca had felt it too; a brief but definite tremor. Peabody, still marching ahead, looked back at her comrades.

"Make haste, gentlemen. We cannot be late." She dug in her purple, velvet bag, took out a small object, looked at it, snapped it shut and dropped it back into her bag.

Danny had seen the object and his face suddenly flashed with fury.

"What is the matter?" Luca asked.

Danny was clearly raging. He ran towards Peabody and hoisted the purple bag from over her shoulder, peering into its pocket.

"What have you done?" he shouted at the tiny woman, his face recoiling from the bag's stench. "How could you?" Throwing the bag towards Luca, he grabbed Peabody by her shoulders and pushed her little body into the rocks.

"What the hell is going on?" Luca shouted, opening the bag quickly and peering in to see its contents. The sight before him made his heart sink and Danny's outburst seemed suddenly tame. He reached in to the bag and lifted out his golden pocket watch. Holding it up, he looked at Peabody, his face the picture of despair. Opening the bag further, the source of the vile odour lay, nestled at the bottom of the purple lining. "The dead blackbird," he said to himself, devastated at the truth of Danny's accusations.

"All this time, she has been working against us," Danny shouted as he held her down against the rocks at the path's edge. "The ground is trembling again. And listen, the waters are angry too. You can hear it."

Luca stood in stunned silence as he pieced together the events in his mind. They had trusted a witch against all the knowledge of her ancestry and she had used them to continue their evil legacy.

The gifted pocket watch had pleased the Earth but now its theft had angered her once more. The king had commissioned the building of the dam to protect the village, and they had willingly destroyed it under her influence. Luca wondered if their home had been flooding overnight, as they slept soundly in the presence of the cause.

His anger, however, was truly sparked by the sight before him of the decaying bird's carcass. He wondered how many times prior to this occasion, she had made an offering to the waters and then callously retrieved it, angering them further and further. She had, perhaps performed this deceitful spell the day Nancy had drowned in the enraged rushing of Thistlewick River.

Luca threw the bag down and ran towards Peabody. He grabbed her from Danny's grip and smashed her again into the rocks, pinning her down with one hand as he raised his other in a fist, and struck her face.

She snarled at him; dark red blood seeping out from between her damaged teeth. He raised his hand again but she placed her finger in the centre of his forehead. A glowing yellow light erupted from her nail and an unimaginable pain spread across Luca's body, forcing him backwards.

Danny reached for his pistol.

"Can I kill her now? I knew we could not trust a witch. Her entire family have brought nothing but chaos to our village." Peabody's eyes widened in fear, glistening with tears as her lips trembled. Luca pushed himself up from the ground, the pain having disappeared as quickly as it had engulfed him. He lurched forwards again, hoping to restrain her before she had chance to cast another spell. As he grabbed her arm, he could see tears flowing down her cheeks as her terrified eyes met his angry stare.

"I have done no wrong!" she cried. "Please. I promise. I have done no wrong."

Luca loosened his grip on her arm and stepped back, looking at the pitiful figure on the ground. She held her hand up to her throbbing face. Her eye was bruising and her cheekbone was visibly broken, swelling as it was in an unnatural mound. Her tiny frame was still crumbled against the rocks but she slowly stood up, toddling awkwardly towards Luca.

"I have done no wrong," she repeated, tears now streaming from her eyes as she looked up at the man before her. She lifted the bag from where it had landed in the fern and bracken of the mountainside. "This poor creature was a sacrifice to the Water Spirits and they gratefully accepted, as you know. That is why, in return, they gave life to the fish, embracing it back into their world."

She took the pocket watch from her bag and held it up. "This," she continued, "was a gift to the Earth. The gold pleased them enormously and the quakes dissipated. The two of you have this knowledge now and you must return the gifts when this is over. However, for today, we need the Waters to be angry, and the Earth to be annoyed, and the Fires to dance with their displeasure. We need all the powers of Magissa's despair to work against each other to destroy her most disturbing creation — the Daughters of the Wind."

Peabody slipped the golden pocket watch back into the pocket of her bag and placed the strap over her head and onto her shoulder once more. She took Luca's hands in hers, still wincing in pain, and through tears she gently smiled.

"I have done no wrong, and everything I have ever done was for you, my brother. My little Baby Joe."

Chapter 20

The pit in the nave was once again filled with the resting creatures, sleeping soundly after their nightly adventures. Their limbs entwined, they cocooned themselves in their folded wings. Typhonia slept, as always, across the altar with Kykie curled at her feet.

This morning, however, Kykie was not sleeping. She had been waiting for this day for many years. Confirmation had arrived several weeks earlier, when a scroll tied with blue ribbon, had been hidden in the wings of an angelic headstone in the Cathedral's grounds. The trusty stone angel had been their go-between for correspondence for decades; ever since a childless young woman had been gifted with a son.

Kykie had not seen Meredith in the meadow that night, at first. She had not heard the sobs of a desperate, heartbroken woman, breeching the curfew, and wishing for death. She had spotted the young woman at the same moment she had heard Typhonia's wings in flight behind her, closing in on her betrayal.

With just moments to decide her actions, Kykie had placed the sleeping baby in the tall grass and flown towards the petrified woman.

"The king must find him." Kykie had said. "He will be yours, but the king must find him."

As Typhonia approached quickly, Kykie had blurted out directions to the whereabouts of an injured young girl on the forest floor. Meredith had, for some reason, trusted the feared creature. She had searched the forest for the injured girl, finding a pool of blood, but no signs of a body. Weeks later, just as the harpy had predicted, she had been gifted with the baby boy and she named him *Luca*.

And so was conceived a bizarre friendship; Meredith saved from her misery, and Kykie finding a longed-for link to the human world.

The latest scroll had simply said a date and time. The date had now arrived and the time was fast approaching. She knew what she needed to do. It was simply a matter of waiting.

Chapter 21

Peabody resumed her march to the mountain's peak as the two men stood dumbstruck.

"Phoebe!" Luca shouted after her. "You are Phoebe?"

The little lady stopped. It had been a long time since anyone had used her name. She turned and looked at her brother.

"Yes," she confirmed, simply. "I am. But we cannot discuss this now. We need to keep going."

"Phoebe, please," Luca shouted, running to catch up to her. "I am so sorry."

She turned around and smiled at him warmly.

"We need to keep going," she said simply, before continuing her walk.

The men began to follow, quickly, still in shock from the revelation. The three moved quickly, Luca and Danny often struggling to keep up with Peabody's impressive pace. By mid-morning they had reached the summit and each stood for a moment, taking in the view around them. Danny took a step towards their small guide.

"Peabody, I am so sorry for doubting your intentions. I did not know the plan." She nodded, not saying a word.

Luca looked at her bruised face, overcome with guilt. "I am so very sorry. Are you quite well?" He put his arm around her and she nodded again, putting her arms around his waist in a tight embrace as he hugged her little body. "Where do we need to go next, Phoebe?"

She smiled up at him, so glad to be in his presence, and for him to finally know the truth of their connection. She pointed down to the ruins of a once grand cathedral. Much of it was still intact but the roof of the bell-tower had long since been destroyed. Where once a striking doorway had been, were rocks and stones, piled high, creating an effective but crude wall. The building itself was surrounded by a field of gravestones enclosed with wrought iron fencing. Many were small and simple crosses whilst others stood proudly as elaborately crafted monuments.

"Is this the Harpy's lair?" Luca asked. Peabody nodded.

"What? We are actually going to their *lair*?" Danny shrieked. "Is that absolutely necessary?"

Peabody laughed at the fear in his voice. "No need to panic, Sir Daniel. It is daylight, after all, although we must hurry. We have but one hour before darkness falls."

"It is still morning," Luca pointed out.

"Ah, yes," Peabody agreed, "and a fine morning it is. But today is a very special day. Today our lovely full moon will travel across the bright blue skies and for several minutes, its path will align perfectly with the Sun until our great light source is fully obscured. It will become very cold and very dark. Day will become night, you see? And what do our harpy-foe like to do at night?" She smiled with glee at the looks of amazement on the faces of her comrades. "They fly!"

The path down the mountainside was clear and winding, and it did not take long before they reached the bottom. Soon, the ground beneath them was level and they made their way to the graveyard.

The cathedral was a huge building and Luca was surprised to see the detail and care that had clearly gone into its construction. Each corner was decorated with menacing gargoyles, each wall carved with effigies, and great stained-glass windows still survived, each depicting an elaborate and colourful scene.

"When was this built?" he asked, having had no knowledge of its existence prior to seeing the king's map.

"Many centuries ago," Peabody replied. "The first king of Thistlewick recognised the unexpected need, when the curse had begun its evil. I believe there was a sudden requirement for a burial place as the dead began to outnumber the living, though its construction was not completed in his lifetime. Of course, it has been used since, though few dare to bury their loved ones here now."

"I had not quite realised the extent of the losses," Danny said. "How many died?"

Peabody looked saddened as she met his gaze. "Hundreds," she replied. "Many were killed when the quakes began, injured beyond recovery as the Earth destroyed the grounds and buildings. The cracks in her crust made way for the flowing waters, where survivors of the tremors cruelly drowned in masses, so sudden was the flooding. Some were burned alive, and of course, others were picked off by Kataigida and her colony."

Looking now at the solemn field of headstones, the men began to comprehend the magnitude of tragedy the village had encountered. Peabody could read their thoughts in their sombre expression.

"Sadly, yes," she answered their unspoken deductions, "Magissa has a lot to answer for. Now, Sir Daniel, you must go a little way up that hill," she ordered, pointing to an area behind the bell-tower. "Gather dried leaves and twigs, whatever you can find, and build the biggest fire you can muster. Luca, please do the same at the old entrance way." She looked at the magnificent building, appearing ever-so-slightly anxious at the task ahead. "And I will obscure the windows."

The men headed off in opposite directions. Peabody made her way into the graveyard, seeking a particular headstone. Once she had found it, she read the words engraved in the stone and stroked her fingers across the name. *Greta.*

"Mama," she whispered. "I need your help."

Peabody opened her purple bag and took out a small, clay pot. Using her fingers she scraped dried earth from the ground around her mother's grave, filling the pot until it overflowed. She was pleased to see two small fires as she made her way to the cathedral walls. Luca and Danny had clearly succeeded in her bidding.

Peabody set down her bag and the clay pot on the ground next to her. She took a great handful of the crumbling dirt and held it tight, whispering into her cupped fingers, her eyes closed in concentration.

Danny and Luca stood together and watched as her fingers opened one by one and the ball of black dirt circled around her palm. The circle grew larger, swirling above her hand like a minute whirlwind. It grew and grew, more of the soil rising from the pot until it circled her entire body. She held her arms out, gesturing at the building before her, and the whirlwind followed her gaze, climbing up the walls and circling wider and wider.

The ground beneath their feet began to tremble as great mounds of earth, from her mother's grave began hurtling into the air, joining the mass of circling darkness now surrounding the cathedral. Peabody began to slowly step backwards, away from the swirling creation, as it grew denser and moved faster with each step. She waved to the men to follow her and they retreated into the graveyard, crouching behind the grave of Greta.

Chapter 22

Kykie had been watching keenly as the windows had darkened. It was time. She slid off the edge of the altar and stood at its side, stroking Typhonia's cheek until her eyes gently opened.

"The Sun is setting, my lady."

Typhonia stretched out her limbs and rose from the altar. She did not feel well rested, but instructed Kykie to rouse the others from their pit.

Outside, Peabody, Luca and Danny began to feel the air chill. They looked up briefly at the Moon's path as its edge had met that of the Sun, creating a celestial figure of eight.

"Do not look directly at it," Peabody warned. "It will blind you."

"Have you seen this happen before?" Danny asked, amazed at the occurrence.

"No, Sir Daniel." She giggled. "The last recorded incident of this, over Thistlewick, was three hundred and sixty-seven years ago. Its recurrence has been a long time coming. I am not quite that old."

"Three hundred and sixty-seven years ago?" Danny asked. "The harpies were in existence then and the treaty in place. Was it not? They cannot have mistaken it for night time then or they would not still be an active enemy?"

"That is right, Sir Daniel," Peabody agreed. "I imagine they did not wake the last time. It does only last for several minutes."

Daniel looked concerned.

"What makes you so certain they will wake this time?"

Peabody smiled,

"Ah! This time we are prepared. During the last occurrence the villagers did not know the reasons behind the sudden darkening of the sky. It is well documented in the archives as causing much panic, by all accounts. However, times have changed. The heavens have been studied and observed. The paths of the stars have been mapped. This time we are of an understanding not only of what will happen, but when, and that knowledge has been passed to our ally within the cathedral walls."

"What ally do you speak of?" Luca asked.

"Shh. We must now be quiet."

She reached into her bag and lifted out the golden pocket watch and decaying black bird. Holding one in each hand she raised them into the air and focussed on the bell-tower. "Any minute now," she advised as the ground trembled again.

The demonic women stretched their wings, preparing for their nightly hunt.

"It is our time once more, my dears," Typhonia announced. "Now go, and for goodness' sake, bring back something more than mice and pigeons. I am sick of the sight and smell of them. Fly now. Hunt well!"

The creatures launched into the air, each clambering to ascend the bell-tower for their nocturnal freedom. They hurtled into the skies, each going towards the mountain, each aiming to reach Thistlewick quickly in the hope that some poor soul had mistakenly breached curfew. Six winged monsters, flying with relish, higher and higher, not seeing the three figures crouching beneath them; the odour of the rotting bird masking their scent.

The path of the great Moon now completely encompassed the rays of the Sun and day had truly become night; if only for a matter of minutes. Its orbit continued and soon glimmers of light fought their way forwards, the sky brightening quickly.

A huge tremble roared beneath the trio in the graveyard as the Earth shook with angrier outbursts. Luca, Danny and Peabody held on to Greta's gravestone as their bodies were shaken in the quake. Desperately trying to keep his balance, Danny looked up to the sky in horror.

"They are coming back!" he cried.

Luca looked up too, seeing the six monstrous women hurtling towards them, their wings flapping furiously. Danny covered his head with his arms, thinking of his pregnant wife and the child he would never see. Peabody placed her hands on his clenched fingers.

"It is too late for them, Sir Daniel. There is no need to be afraid. They will not fly faster than the Moon."

She was right, of course. Within moments a discord of devilish howls erupted from the skies. It was their eagle-like wings that succumbed first to the Sun's rays. Each horned tip began sparkling with flames which ate through their grey flesh until black, burnt remnants left them flightless. Each revolting creature, in turn, fell from the skies, their skin cracking and burning — melting from their bones as they screamed in terror. As each charred corpse smashed against the ground, an explosion of powdery, silver ash erupted. Caught by the breeze, it was whisked away forever.

Danny let out a huge sigh of relief.

"You did it, Peabody. You bloody did it," he cried, squeezing her into a grateful embrace. Luca grabbed the pair in a huge hug, laughing with absolute elation. The tiny woman, encompassed in the gratitude of the men, was not celebrating quite so soon.

"I am afraid there is one more that we need to destroy. But only one. Their leader does not fly with them. She is still in the walls of the cathedral." She paused as she looked at the structure, still in darkness from the whirling soil. "And she will be mad!"

Chapter 23

Typhonia paced the nave as the ground shook beneath her bare feet. The noise of the shaking stone building was deafening and she had to shout to be heard.

"What is happening? They had calmed the Earth. Why is she vexed again?"

Kykie shook her head.

"Something is not as it should be," she continued. "I can feel it."

She turned around, walking towards the base of the old bell-tower. Each step brought with it a sudden and increasing fatigue. She felt a weakening in her bones and a sense of panic began growing in her. Looking up to the open space above the lip of the bell-tower, her face dropped in horror as she saw a bright blue sky above her.

"No!" she cried. "It cannot be!"

Kykie scuttled behind the altar. She knew she would now witness a rage like no other and she certainly did not wish to be close by. The cry from Typhonia pierced through the building, echoing around the trembling walls. She ran to the altar and slammed her fist onto the stone, just as another mighty tremor roared beneath her. The altar cracked under her hand, the break travelling like lightening across the top surface, down the front and onto the stone floor. Typhonia screamed as the action broke the bones of her hand. She felt a searing pain for the first time in four centuries, and she knew then, her powers were fading. Another violent tremble and the crack in the stone floor, travelled further, deeper and wider until a huge crevice cascaded across the length of the room.

Typhonia glared at Kykie,

"This is your doing!" She shouted. Kykie stood to her full height and nodded, no longer willing to live fearfully of the woman before her.

"We are not for this world, Typhonia. We have tortured lives enough."

Peabody held the golden pocket watch above her head, willing the anger of the Earth to do her bidding. As the ground shook, the fires raged and the blackened soil whirled around the cathedral, the elements fought each other in violent outbursts. The power of their forces was utterly terrifying but Peabody did not falter. She had her brother by her side and the will of her late mother running through her veins. She would end this curse once and for all.

With another almighty quake, a great crack shot down the stones of the bell-tower. It ran down the side of the building, shattering each stained-glass window in turn, until the entire eastern wall collapsed away from the body of the cathedral. With the inside now exposed, Peabody grabbed the sword from Danny's holster and charged towards the building.

"No!" Luca cried, running after her, but she was determined. She moved so rapidly, in spite of her form, that Luca could not stop her. She was quickly at the side of the cathedral, scrambling over the shattered ruins and shielding her head from falling stones with her free arm. Luca followed as quickly as he could, while Danny hesitantly pursued, unsure whether the inside or outside of the cathedral posed a greater threat to their lives.

Typhonia crouched behind the remnants of the altar, her wings no real barrier from the sunlight which flooded the room, but she folded them around her for comfort. She could feel her strength ebbing away. Her sisters had broken the treaty, albeit mistakenly, and Magissa's gift to her now drifted from her pores. Encompassed in her pain, she did not hear the tiny footsteps of the little lady she had mutilated all those years ago. Aware of her toes becoming singed, she opened her wings a little to pull her knees closer and spare her feet the burning. As she did, her eyes locked on the disfigured face of Greta's daughter.

"You little witch!" Typhonia cried. "I will destroy you." She tried to push herself up from the floor, but her energy had faded with her powers.

Peabody smiled at her.

"Oh, Typhonia, you destroyed me many years ago. Look at me. What more can you do?" She raised the sword above her head and plunged it deep into Typhonia's chest.

"That is for my mother!" She said gleefully. She twisted the sword and pushed it in further before pulling it out, allowing the pitiful, dying creature to slump to the side. She watched as the harpy's skin began to crack and blacken, smouldering in the light until nothing remained.

Luca had witnessed Typhonia's demise and finally reached Peabody, having clambered over the mounds of rubble. He was shocked and impressed in equal measure, by his sister's heroic act and he picked her up in a giant hug and span her around.

Their celebrations were brief, however, as the fires had reached the building and were now burning along the crevice of the floor.

"Come on, we need to get out of here," Luca said, hurrying Peabody away from the growing flames. Danny climbed into the remnants of the cathedral, shielding his eyes from the billowing smoke. He squinted to see two figures moving towards him and was hugely relieved to see Luca and Peabody. As the ground shook and the fires raged, Danny shouted at them to move swiftly.

Keeping a close watch on the pair's progress, a movement behind them caught Danny's eye. Peering through the fog of black smoke, he could see the naked figure of a woman and the vague outline of a wing.

"Look out, there's another one!" he cried, pulling out his pistol from under his robe. Luca looked behind him, seeing the winged woman, and hoped Danny was as good a shot as the king had believed. But Peabody's face dropped.

"No, Danny!" she shouted. "Not her. Not Kykie." She ran towards the last living harpy. Kykie had remained hidden behind the cathedral's giant pulpit until the smoke had shielded her from the Sun's rays. But as the black fog had grown denser, she had been forced from her hiding place, and into the open.

"Not her!" Peabody shouted again as she stumbled towards her brother's saviour.

Danny had not heard her desperate pleas. The shot rang out. His aim was faultless. Without an obstacle in its path, it would almost certainly have hit the harpy's chest. Instead though, it hit Peabody between her shoulder blades and she fell to the rubble beneath her.

She wasn't moving. Her tiny body had fallen hard on the rocky ground. Luca, Danny and Kykie rushed to her side. With the ancient building burning and crumbling around them, Luca picked up his sister in his arms not knowing if she was dead or alive, but being absolutely certain that they needed to get out. He ordered Danny to cover Kykie with his robes and guide her towards the graveyard, uncertain as to why they were protecting this creature, but trusting Peabody's judgement.

They clambered over broken blocks and mounds of scorching rubble, weaving between flickering flames until the fresh air of the graveyard allowed respite from their coughing.

Greta's grave was now a gaping hole, revealing the aged wooden coffin as the earth from its cavity still circled the burning cathedral. Luca laid Peabody's tiny frame on the fresh grass by its side. He thought he had felt her moving as he had carried her, but could not be sure. He stroked her face and gently shook her arm.

"Phoebe!" he pleaded, tears rolling down his cheeks. Danny looked on horrified, praying she was alive, and that his shot had not taken from them the little woman who had become a good friend.

"Phoebe, please!" Luca said again.

Her eyes opened slowly. Seeing Luca before her, she smiled.

"Baby Joe," she said. She looked around her, seeing Danny's worried face and Kykie peering out from under the dark robe.

"Oh, Sir Daniel, do not fret."

"I am so sorry," he cried. "I am so, so sorry."

Luca grabbed Peabody's purple bag and thrust it at Danny.

"Take this. Do something useful and return the gifts before Thistlewick is destroyed. And take her with you," he ordered, gesturing at Kykie. "She can stay in the cottage until nightfall."

Danny took the bag without a word and guided Kykie away, overcome with guilt. He would re-bury the blackbird's body at the riverbank, and return the golden pocket watch to the circular wall they had built for the Earth. He would do this for Peabody.

Dark, red blood seeped from the wound in Peabody's back as she looked at her brother's concerned face. Luca could not stop the tears from falling. He knew she could not survive this. There were so many questions he had wanted to ask her, so many answers he had needed to know and so much admiration for her that he wanted to express. But looking at her dying body, he could not say a word. He took off his overcoat, laid it over her shivering shoulders, and held her hand in his.

"I was not always like this, Baby Joe," she said, her voice weak. "Typhonia killed our mama and your father, John. I knew she would kill you next. I was born from evil, but you were born from love and she could not stand the thought of that. I took you and ran, casting a blinding spell behind us to prevent us from being seen by evil.

"Kykie could see us though and I knew her heart was good. I gave you to her, with the golden pocket watch, blessed with my love to keep you calm and stop your cries. It broke my heart to let go of you. I was unsure if she could keep you from Typhonia, but I knew that I could not. I believed I could slow her down, though. I could give Kykie more time to get you to safety.

"Typhonia enjoyed each sickening hour it took her to turn me into this. She thought I was as good as dead. But our mama's spirit took away my pain and helped me to heal as completely as could be hoped for.

"Kykie sent help — a lady from the village, but I hid from her in my grief. I did not need help. I had my little cottage, warmth and food. Each night I would think of you. I hoped you were safe and wished that you were happy."

Luca's face was wet with tears. He had never known a love so pure.

"You were mistaken when you told Typhonia she had destroyed you, sweetheart," he told her. He sobbed as he stroked her bruised face. "Against her will, she made you. You are the strongest and most beautiful soul I have ever known and I am honoured to call you, my sister."

She reached out to wipe away his tears and whispered,

"Go to sleep, Baby Joe,
No more tears must flow.
Time to rest, Baby Joe,

To Dreamland you must go."

She squeezed his hand lightly but Luca sobbed as he felt all her strength slowly fading away. Her eyes closed with her final breath, and she was gone.

Chapter 24

The fires raged on and the Earth continued its ever-increasing trembling with no consideration for the sorrow engulfing Luca's heart. He could stay no longer, so close to the epicentre of the elements' rage. He gently lowered his sister's body into their mother's grave. A sudden breeze brushed over his shoulders as all the circling soil and earth began to drift away from the ruins of the cathedral, and return to Greta's resting place, burying Phoebe's body with her mother for eternity.

Luca reluctantly sobbed his goodbyes, walking alone through the gravestones and tall grass. He thought back to the events of the last few days. All that they had encountered and all that they had done. Though he was angry at Danny for Phoebe's death, he knew beneath his sorrow, he was not to blame. Danny had not known of Kykie and was simply trying to end the years of torment committed by the Daughters of the Wind, just as he was now doing with the Water Spirits and the powers of the Earth. Luca wondered what Phoebe's plan had been to calm the forces of the Fire. They would have to be tamed too, without the knowledge and power of his sister. He had almost reached the graveyard's gated entrance when an engraving on a large boulder caught his eye.

Here lies Magissa, who rests, not in peace.
Her spirit still haunting, her wrath not released.
No spoken word uttered could answer her quest,
Though written word nestles, where written words rest.

The truth never known of the love lost, in life,
Her body lays here, her soul caught in strife.

"The truth never known?!" Luca pondered as he stared intently at the crude engraving. "Where written words rest?" A realisation struck him. Magic and sorcery may travel down the female line, but he was still Greta's son. Her strength and determination were within him. He knew what he needed to do.

Darkness had fallen over the village of Thistlewick. The streets were empty, the residents still abiding by a curfew no longer necessary. Luca walked past his house, glancing at the upstairs window where Weavles sat; waiting for his safe return. Just a little longer, hopefully, Luca thought.

He turned the corner into Main Street, and was surprised to see the front door of Angus's house wide open. He saw Florence drifting out of the opening, her eyes glazed and unfocussed. Her long, black hair hung down like greasy drapes, wafting across her nightgown. She carried a single candle, and with bare feet, made careful steps along their garden pathway. Luca was preparing to stop her but he saw Angus run out of the house after her, the panic in his face disappearing as he saw her figure in their garden. He took her softly by the arm, guided her back in to the house without saying a word and closed the door on the world.

Luca heard footsteps behind him and turned quickly to see Danny walking towards him, his expression still a picture of guilt and mourning.

"Is it done?" Luca asked.

Danny nodded. "The waters have already begun to recede and the tremors are calming." Luca nodded back. The thought had not occurred to him until now but he realised he hadn't felt trembling for a few hours.

"I am truly sorry, Luca. I... I am."

Luca put his hand on Danny's shoulder,

"You are not to blame. She knew that, and I understand too."

Danny sighed, comforted by the words but knowing in his heart he would never forgive himself.

"What of the harpy?" Luca asked. "Is she safe?"

"Yes. She seemed quite happy in the cottage. She told me what had happened all those years ago." He shook his head, still shocked at the horror.

The men looked around at their home, glad to see the elements had not caused too much destruction. The roof of the old distillery had collapsed entirely, leaving a gaping hole in the side of the building. The old copper stills, now damaged beyond repair, were strewn across the floor and surrounded by chipped bricks and charred timbers. Several painted fences lay in the streets, blocking the pathways rather than surrounding pretty gardens, and the old fountain was cracked, leaking a trickle of water across the lane. The damage would take time to repair, but that seemed to be all.

"What are we to do now?" Danny asked. "Without our wise friend for guidance."

"We are going to the manor," Luca said. "We need to find something."

The king's men had let the weary travellers pass without question, eager to hear of the outcome of their quest, but there was no time to tell their tale without one final act.

"King William is still fighting!" one of the guards had revealed to them. "Doctor Carter is still here with him." They were glad of this news. They needed a little more time with his protection.

Danny, at his request, led Luca to the grand library held within the walls of Thistlewick Manor. Luca immediately began to scan the floor-to-ceiling shelves, packed with leather-bound books.

"Oh! This could take a while!" he sighed, and started reading the spines of each book in turn. "I had not realised the collection would be quite so extensive."

"What are we looking for, exactly?" Danny asked, as he turned his head to read several titles.

"Diaries, journals," Luca answered, "anything that looks like a four-hundred-year-old, hand written book."

"All right," Danny nodded, beginning the search at one side of the enormous room. "But to what end?"

"We need to find out what happened to the brother of the first king of Thistlewick. It was Fergal's disappearance that led to the curse."

"Ah, yes." Danny remembered Luca telling him the story when they had first begun their journey. "Magissa thought King Frederick had killed him."

"That's right," Luca said as he fingered his way along book after book. "Her spirit will not rest until she knows the truth."

"What if her suspicions were correct?" Danny asked, still looking. "That would surely vindicate the curse forever?"

Luca shook his head. "I am hoping that will not be the case but I honestly do not believe it will be of consequence either way, as long as it is the truth."

"Are you certain the diary will be here?" Danny asked, daunted by the number of titles they would need to eliminate.

"Not at all, but let us hope so. This is, after all, where written words rest."

They searched for hours, their knees sore from crouching down to view the lower shelves, their shoulders aching from reaching up to the volumes set high above their heads.

"Here!" Danny suddenly shouted. "I have found something."

Luca rushed over. Together they thumbed through the pages, reading short sections. Each part told of faraway places, unheard of towns and newly discovered villages across the land.

"This is Fergal's diary," Luca agreed. "Well done, Danny." They read the final entry.

I journeyed back to her in spring. She is blooming now, her belly swelling with my child. Her company enraptures me and I am saddened further each time I have to say goodbye. I cannot stay away from my brother for too long though. He is not strong and he worries night and day with constant fears of our father. He is convinced the miserable old man is searching for us, seeking revenge for our abandonment. But I care not if he is. He will not be welcomed here and I would sooner kill him than return, though I miss Mother dearly.

I will journey again in the morning, to visit my love. And when I return, I will tell Frederick of her. She will need to travel here soon before our child is born, and he deserves to know first. She has beautiful and powerful magic within her though he need not be afraid.

"He need not be afraid!" Luca repeated, with his eyebrows raised. "That is quite the false prophecy!"

Danny laughed. "Indeed."

"Damn it. This tells us nothing," Luca said, thumbing through the subsequent empty pages. "What happened then, Fergal? Where did you go?" Luca bent down to replace the diary in the empty slot, his knees cracking as he did so. "You would find it on a low shelf, runt." Danny rolled his eyes.

As Luca pushed the book into the shelf, it hit against an obstruction, leaving the spine hanging out over the edge. Luca pulled it back out; peering into the void to see what had been dislodged. Sticking out from behind the neighbouring volumes was a leather-bound book, facing outwards. It had clearly been pushed to the back of the shelving and concealed. He lifted it out, brushed the thick layer of dust from its edges and wiped his hand over the black leather. There was no title on the cover or spine. No embossed lettering revealing its contents.

Luca raised his eyebrows at Danny. "Promising!" he said with slight hesitation.

A black silk ribbon was wrapped around the book, tied in a tight knot at the pages' edge. Danny took out a small knife from the pocket of his breeches and slid it under the ribbon, snapping it in half. Luca opened the cover. He could see the pages were hand written and was certain he held in his hands the diary of King Frederick.

Fergal left again today, on his merry travels. I know not what he seeks when we have all we need here. This perfect manor house has ample room, he need not feel unwelcome. I wonder that he has a lady friend somewhere in the world, but he has not disclosed this to me.

I fret when he is away. I know he thinks me foolish, but I worry for his safety. I am always so pleased when he returns. I hope he is not gone long this time.

My men have almost completed the east wing now and I hope to gift this part of the house to Fergal. Perhaps with his own space, he will not feel so compelled to stay away.

It has been three weeks since Fergal said farewell. He has journeyed for longer but I feel a weakness in my heart with this absence, as though an injury or illness has accosted him. I fear I will feel uneasy until his safe return, whenever that might be.

It has been the worst of days. My brother has returned and I ought to be rejoicing but he is not himself. Not even a shadow of him. I had told him this would happen. Over and over, I voiced my concerns but he scoffed at my words. It was not safe to wander the lands alone. I am unsure of the details for he cannot utter a word, so swollen is his face with bruising. His eyes can barely open. Each bone seems broken. If he still breathes at sunrise, I would be happily surprised. My lovely Violet, and her maid are with him now, tending to wounds I believe will not heal, and supressing unimaginable pain. I can but hope the morning brings good news.

I sat by Fergal's bedside from sunrise until sunset. He was drifting between a feverish sleep and a frightful lucidity. He was able to speak a little today and confessed to finding love, but his eyes filled with tears at the thought of not seeing her again or meeting their unborn child. He made me swear an oath to never reveal to her that he had died a coward; to never reveal how his life had ended. So desperate was he, that I made the promise before knowing the truth myself.

I should not have been shocked when he told me, but to have had my worst fears asserted, horrified me. He had been staying in a tavern and was in a deep sleep when the door to his room burst open. He had stood up and reached for his sword but in that very moment, realised he could not use it. Two figures had stood in the doorway. One was our father against whom he would have used any given weapon with no hesitation. The other, though, was our lovely mother, sobbing at the thought of what was to happen.

Our monstrous father, now old but still so strong and more vengeful than ever, struck Fergal over and over. Fergal would not strike back, nor use his sword for he would never allow our mother to witness her son becoming a killer. Father had always hidden from her, the violence he used against us. Though his behaviour towards his children was abhorrent, he was never cruel to Mother and she had always loved him. She cannot be blamed for thinking we had selfishly abandoned our parents.

When our father was certain that Fergal was dead, they left. But he was mistaken, and so began my brother's long and painful journey home to warn me.

And now, I must keep this secret, and word of Fergal's brief survival must never be spoken. Our father would ensure he did not make that mistake more than once and would trace him back here.

I made a pledge to my dear brother, through my tears, as he took his final breath. He is free now of our father's anger, but I am not. I will keep my promise forever to conceal his demise and ensure the attack cannot be repeated. Not for my own sake, but the safety of my children. He would not hesitate to harm them. Of that I am certain.

"Oh, my word!" Danny shouted. "Four hundred and fifty years! Four hundred and fifty years, Luca, and the first king had not so much as laid a finger on his brother. He was keeping a bloody promise!"

Luca nodded. "So it would seem," he said, dazed by the revelation.

"That witch!"

"That is not entirely fair, Danny. Their father played a hand in this."

"Well, quite," Danny agreed. "Magissa was certainly the catalyst though, in the ensuing misery."

With that, Luca came back to his senses. "Magissa. That is right. We need to let her know. The fires will descend with the king's last breath if we do not gift her with this knowledge. Make haste, Danny. There is one last journey ahead of us."

"Where are we going?" Danny called after Luca, following him out of the grand library.

"We need to go back to the graveyard." Luca shouted back.

Danny sighed, "Oh, for goodness' sake, not again!"

They were exhausted as they reached the sacred ground once more. Flames still spat out of the cathedral's remnants but the ground no longer shook. Luca pointed to the engraved boulder.

"Here she lies," he said to Danny.

The men worked together to clear the earth out from around the giant rock before lifting it out of its hollow. Her body had not been encased in a coffin, and the men were shocked to see her skeletal remains discarded in the ground. Her aged skull revealed an extensive, gaping fracture along the temple and they wondered if the injury was present prior to her neglectful burial. Luca placed King Frederick's diary into the cavity beside her and they pushed her headstone back into position, patting down the earth around it.

"Fergal was not killed by his brother," Luca said to the stone, hoping the spirit of Magissa could hear his words. "Nor did he die a coward, as he so believed. He died with honour, shielding his mother from a lifetime of viewing her eldest son as a killer and protecting his brother's children from their wicked grandfather. That is not weakness. That is great strength. He loved you and would have been a good father to your son. I hope you can now rest in peace, Magissa."

Instantly, Danny and Luca heard a gushing of water from the high ground above the cathedral. The water rushed in great streams down the hillside, washing away the flames as the sun rose behind the mountain. The flowing tides were substantial and Danny began to take great paces away, fearing it would flood the graveyard. Luca did not move though, knowing the elements were no longer seeking chaos. He bowed his head gratefully as the streams disappeared into the crevice left in the cracked earth.

"Peabody was right, again," Danny declared. "We did need the waters to be agreeable, after all."

Luca smiled at her memory and nodded.

"We can go home now, Sir Daniel."

"Danny," the small man corrected.

Chapter 25

Meredith sat silently in the armchair next to the king's bed. She had been keeping vigil day and night, watching each painful breath he forced. Doctor Carter had kept close by through the days, but there was little he could do, and even less the king would allow.

She stroked his grey hair, wincing in empathy at each painful breath he took.

His eyes slowly opened. Seeing his love gazing at him and feeling her touch, a sense of calm drove away his fears for the first time in many years.

"Could I have done more?" he asked her.

She shook her head.

"You did everything you could for your people," she reassured him. "The curse was mighty but you suppressed its magic more than anyone before you."

He smiled at her and held her fingers.

"I mean, could I have done more to secure your hand?"

She closed her eyes as tears escaped them and softly shook her head. "I was always yours."

The king squeezed her hand, savouring her touch with burdening sadness, knowing he could not hold on much longer.

He saw a sudden flickering in the flames of the many candles lighting his room. The ever-present gloom encompassing the manor house seemed to fade into the warmth. He thought for a moment that he could hear birdsong in the distance despite the depth of the windowless walls, and then he understood.

"It is done," he suddenly announced. "I can feel it."

Meredith smiled and touched his hand.

"You can go now William, my king, my friend... my love. You can go now."

The king smiled back at her, gazing at her kind face, until the life left his eyes.

Chapter 26

Smoke billowed from the chimney of the little stone cottage in the woods. Though it was a warm day, its resident enjoyed lighting the fire in the cosy sitting room and watching the flames flicker in the grate. She had taken time over the last few days to make the cottage her home, cleaning its contents and airing the rooms. She kept everything in its place though, respecting its previous occupant. She would not, after all, be staying long.

She sat in the armchair next to the fire, wrapped in a long shawl, polishing the silverware. A knock at the door startled her and she instinctively looked through the windows before remembering that the time of day was no longer of consequence. She opened the little window at the top of the door and saw her friend's face smiling back.

"Meredith!" she exclaimed. She had not seen her for many years; the lady having only been free during daylight, where the harpy had only known respite in darkness.

"Kykie, my good friend, it is so good to see you."

Kykie opened the door and gestured for her welcomed guest to enter. They sat at the dining table elated to finally be in each other's company.

"All went to plan, then?" Meredith asked.

"It certainly did. You should be very proud of Luca. Your king, too, was a very clever man. To have researched the movements of the moon, and ensured our little friend was made aware of its significance was a remarkable undertaking."

Meredith smiled at the memory of him.

"Had you known the little girl had survived, Kykie?" she asked.

"I had hoped so, but feared not, given Typhonia's treatment of her. The king must have been told of the little lady in the woods and pieced it together, where we had failed. I wonder if he had known of her connection to your dear boy."

Meredith shook her head,

"The king kept many secrets, but he would not have kept that from me, or from Luca. There was a detail of the sinister history that I was unaware of, but must have been known to the king; a certain light cast on it through his last will and testament. King Frederick had two children, did he not?" Kykie nodded. "I had always believed they had been victims of the revolt. That appears now to have not been the case."

"That is true, thankfully." Kykie confirmed. "Queen Violet was slain by a man named Matthew. But he spared the children. Thomas was seven years old when he witnessed the murder of his mother. Prudence was just three. When Magissa arrived at the manor house, several days later, she discovered them, clinging to their mother's body. She entrusted them to her sister, Hazel, who raised them with her own children. There are those who would have you believe Magissa was a vengeful, evil witch, but she was not entirely ruthless.

"After all of their misfortune, the children were incredibly lucky to have been gifted to Hazel. She was a kind and very gentle woman. It became clear to her, as the children grew, that Prudence remembered nothing of that dreadful night. She became a very happy, contented little girl.

"Thomas, however, was a very troubled and silent little soul. He would not utter a single word to anyone, about any matter, not even his sister. Hazel feared that he would never forget the events of the revolt, and his memories would lead to a lifetime of unhappiness. She tried many times to release him from his silence but the little boy refused to speak.

"When Prudence was nine, she became engrossed in an argument with Hazel's youngest daughter, Ivy. Prudence had insulted her and Ivy retorted by sniggering at the sad truth that Prudence and her brother were orphans, and that Hazel was not their mother. Thomas, quite unexpectedly, shouted out in anger, crying that their parents had been murdered and they need not be reminded. He sobbed as he described the attack on his mother.

"At thirteen years old, Thomas had finally found his voice. He described, in great detail to Hazel, the memories he held of that night. The slaughter he had witnessed should never have been in the mind of a child and Hazel assured him that his recollections would serve a very special purpose; she would ensure that they did.

"Over the years, Magissa had tried on many occasions to convince Hazel to support her with a counter-curse. She believed that their combined power would be strong enough to banish all remnants of the unruly elements. Hazel, though, refused each plea. She had never embraced the magic within her and now, more than ever, she felt no desire to assist a woman whose actions had caused so much devastation to so many innocent people.

"In time, Magissa's son came of age. He could reign alone, without her overbearing supervision. His first desire as sovereign was to end the village's crippling curse. He had seen the effects of the dark magic and had heard the tales of death and destruction that had preceded the treaty. He had not known then, that the torment had been created by his own mother.

"He was deeply angered when his aunt revealed the truth to him and an argument broke out between mother and son. His fury grew stronger with every sorry excuse she made for her behaviour. Indeed, so enraged was he that the argument turned violent and quickly resulted in Magissa's death. For the rest of his reign, no sign of remorse was ever observed. He ordered his guards to bury her in an unmarked grave. Not once did I see him in the cathedral's grounds, paying any respects to his mother.

"I did once spy Hazel in the graveyard, early one morning, several years after her sister's passing. Following her visit, Magissa's grave was no longer unmarked, though I suspect the motivation for that particular engraving was not remorse."

Meredith looked at her friend fondly as she recounted the witch's tale, saddened by the evil that had penetrated generations long after her demise. But a deeper sorrow suddenly swept over her. "You have made a decision, Kykie; I can see it in your eyes. You are returning to the wind."

Kykie smiled back at her with a deep affection. They had confessed so many of their thoughts to each other, through their secret scrolls, that they would each mourn the other's absence.

"I am," she confessed. "It is where I belong. Kataigida was right, all those centuries ago. Had she been listened to, this nightmare would have been a distant memory now. We were created in anger, never to truly belong here. I have had my time."

A tear fell from Meredith's cheek. She took her friend's hand, knowing this would be their first and last real meeting.

"Thank you, Kykie, for all that you have done. You will be warmly remembered."

Chapter 27

Luca was grateful to wake in his own bed with the tiny weight of Weavles on his chest. She had not left his side for the three days he had been back home in Thistlewick. He stroked her head and she purred with contentment.

"Breakfast, then, madam," he said to her, getting out of bed and making his way down his rickety old stairs.

A knock at the door startled him and he looked back at his old grandfather clock to check the time. Six o'clock.

"Early for visitors!" he said to Weavles who scarpered back up the stairs. He opened the door to see Sir Daniel knocking, a huge smile on his face.

"A girl!" Danny cried, elated. "We have had a baby girl."

Luca's face lit up.

"Well done, Danny! Come in, come in." He shook Danny's hand as the short man stepped inside. "That is good news."

"Thank you. She was born in the early hours of this morning. I wanted you to be the first to know."

Luca smiled at him, thrilled for his good fortune.

"Has she been named?" he asked.

"Yes," Danny paused, hoping Luca would be pleased. "We would like to name her Phoebe, if that would have your approval?"

Luca stepped closer to Danny and hugged his friend.

"It is perfect," he said. "Phoebe. That is a beautiful name."

"In honour of a beautiful soul," Danny said. "She is always in my thoughts."

They shared a pot of tea as Luca poured fresh water into a bowl for Weavles, who was still cowering on the stairs, and scowling at the intruder in her home.

"What now for you, Luca? Has our adventure given you a new appreciation for the quiet life, or lit a flame for excitement?" Danny asked, light-heartedly.

"I have not quite decided." Luca laughed. "Some matters will depend on our new ruler, whoever that might be. I imagine changes will be made which may dictate to us our new lives."

Danny nodded.

"Changes will most certainly be made," he agreed, quite resolutely. "Although there will be no dictating."

Luca looked up from his tea.

"Ah! You know who it is then? Have the council deliberated?"

"I was informed late last night, yes. There was no deliberation necessary, apparently. King William had made a will. He had evidently spent many years researching his family tree to find a suitable heir."

"He was the last in his line though, was he not, or the protection of Magissa's magic would have continued?" Luca asked.

"Sadly, yes and may he rest in peace. He was the last direct descendant of Fergal, and his witch. Fergal's brother

Frederick, however, had two children. We were always led to believe that they had been killed in the revolt but King William, discovered that the rumour of such slaughter was created to protect the children in their new lives. He then traced the line down the generations.

"Thomas, Frederick's son, did not marry. He became a farmer and lived happily alone. He was quite the recluse by all accounts. Frederick's daughter, Prudence, however, married into a family who lived in the village. She had several children and there is one surviving great-great-grandchild."

Luca looked surprised.

"That is good news," he declared. "Someone we are familiar with then?"

"Very," Danny replied, smiling. "I will be crowned at the summer solstice. And you, my friend, will be knighted." Luca had never looked quite so stunned.

"My word, Sir Daniel, if I had known you were to be my future king, I would not have called you an undersized runt," he laughed. "Well, certainly not quite as frequently." He smiled at him, delighted that his former comrade was to become his king. He would be a fair and inspiring monarch.

The men shook hands and Danny left to return to his wife and baby daughter, leaving Luca to get washed and dressed. There was something he needed to do which he could put off no longer.

He stepped out of his front door; nudging the newly-attentive Weavles back inside with his foot. Walking from the edge of the village he saw that repairs had already been carried out on the old distillery, and all the fallen fences were now back in place. Even the old fountain appeared to have been restored to its previous glory, with a gentle spray of water landing gracefully into its small moat. Preparations had clearly begun for the king's funeral. Royal blue ribbons adorned the slender trunks of the neat row of blossom trees that lined the cobbled paving. As he walked towards Main Street, he was struck by the warm weather and sunny sky. A village, once damned, seemed suddenly quite lovely, even in the midst of mourning.

He knocked on a green wooden door and waited patiently, hoping it would be answered. He could hear movement inside the house and heard locks being pulled aside as the door cracked open. A tall and portly man stood in the doorway, his dark hair sticking out at all angles and his unkempt beard tangled around his jaw line.

"Angus," Luca nodded, holding out his hand. The man shook it but looked surprised at his sudden guest.

"I am sorry to trouble you but I wonder if I might see Florence?" Luca asked. Angus furrowed his brow, surprised at the request. "I have a clearer understanding now, of how far reaching our curse truly was," Luca explained. "Certain details may offer her some comfort."

Angus said nothing but allowed him entry and pointed upstairs. Luca noted how broken the man appeared. He felt a tremendous sorrow for his dishevelled host and hoped that his news would assist Angus as well as bringing some small solace to his wife.

"She is in her room," Angus sighed, "although you will get no response from her. She is no longer present in our world. She has not been for some time."

Luca followed Angus up the stairway and into a tiny back-bedroom. The room was gloomy despite the open drapes, and a stagnant odour emanated from Florence's ghostly figure. She sat motionless in a wooden rocking chair, staring at the view from her window; a tray of untouched food resting on the table beside her. Still dressed in the dark nightgown she had been wearing several nights ago, her appearance was a far stretch from the young woman he had known as Nancy's closest friend.

Luca took a small wooden stool from next to the bed and placed it beside her rocking chair. He sat down, close to her, hoping to catch her eye. Her gaze out of the window did not falter. Luca stood up and moved to the window, looking out at the view that greeted him: the Thistlewick River. *Of course*, he thought.

He sat back down next to her and took her hand in his as Angus watched on, keen to see if it sparked any life in his haunted wife.

"Florence," Luca whispered. There was no acknowledgment. "Florence, do you remember me?"

He waited for a response but there was nothing.

"Florence, I am here to tell you that you were right. There was a little girl in the river on the day that Nancy drowned. Not a real little girl, but the image of one, created by malicious waters. I am certain of that now."

Florence did not move. Her vacant expression was dreadful to behold. Luca thought back to the lively young lady she had been before the accident. He hoped he would one day see that vibrancy again, and imagined that Angus had lived with those thoughts daily.

"You are not to be blamed for what happened that day," he reassured her. "Nancy loved you and would not have wanted you to live in such sadness."

Though she remained silent and still, a single tear rolled down her cheek. Luca stood up and kissed her forehead, then followed Angus back down the stairs of the little house. Angus opened the front door but stopped Luca before he could step back outside.

"Thank you, Luca," he said, kindly. Luca smiled and nodded but felt an awful guilt in his stomach for blaming Florence for Nancy's death. In moments of his darkest grief, he had wished her ill and now, having witnessed the extent of her demise, regretted those awful desires.

"What will you do now, Luca?" Angus asked. "I heard of your quest. There is talk of nothing else in the village, if truth be told. Does your success at taming the fires not leave you rather short on orders for wood? There will be no more need to keep a fire alive in the cellar of the manor house, so they say."

Luca laughed. "Yes, I have rather managed to put myself out of business, I suppose." He looked out towards Main Street, remembering the once thriving village as it had been before the king's health had started to deteriorate. "Well Angus, I was thinking that the village needs its most important asset back."

Angus looked confused and Luca laughed, patting the man on the back, as he stepped out of the doorway.

"I am going to re-open the Thistlewick Inn, my friend," Luca declared. "And, when I do, I will give you a pitcher of ale on the house." Angus smiled as Luca made his way down the little garden path. Before he reached the gateway he shouted back, "All will be welcome, Angus. Florence will be well again and we will raise our glasses to Nancy. We will raise them, too, for my late sister, Phoebe, without whom the village would certainly have been destroyed. We will drink to their memories, Angus, and then we will stop looking back and start truly living. Better times are coming."

EPILOGUE
November 1373

The corridors of Thistlewick Manor stretched out across the entire length of the huge building. Each one led to room after countless room. Peter ran along, carrying in his shaking hands, the two diaries he desperately needed to destroy. He forced each oak door open in turn certain that there would be a chamber in such a large building, which had a lit fire, even at this late hour. The winter had been harsh, and an icy, stone building would surely be unbearable without some warmth crackling from within. Yet each room seemed colder than the last as he searched frantically, each fireplace empty, but for ash and dust.

"My word," he muttered to himself as a sorrowful understanding came to him. "W*e left them to freeze."*

The village had been wrongly ostracising their king, and the family had been cut off from each and every trade of its people. They had clearly been struggling on through the harsh season without fuel enough to light their fires. A dreadful guilt stirred in the pit of his stomach at the thought of them spending night after night shivering in their beds. He wondered if they had also been denied food and felt a sickening shame for his involvement in shunning their monarch. *"Those poor children,"* he thought.

He ran down another spiralling staircase to yet another long and unlit corridor. The narrow windows offered a little light but this served only to stir a fresh panic in Peter. He was taking too long in his task. He briefly considered concealing the books on his person and destroying them once safely in his own home, but should they be discovered on him, they would instantly reveal the terrible mistakes of the night. No, he thought to himself, the items must never leave this manor.

His thoughts were still reeling in shock at the sudden actions of Samuel as he ran further along the corridor. He knew there had been a deep-rooted loathing of the man he blamed for his daughter's death, but he had not displayed even a notion of murderous intentions on their journey to the manor. It had, after all, been Samuel who had restrained Matthew in his interrogation of the king. It became clear to Peter that the loss of a child could turn even the gentlest of souls into a vengeful being. When Samuel had seen his daughter captured in the talons of a monstrous harpy the image must have burned into his soul. Blame had to lie somewhere. If only Peter had shared the revelations he had read with Samuel as well as with Matthew, they would not now be in this predicament.

Opening the first of many doors on the long passageway, Peter looked inside, quickly assessing that this room, like the others, had no lit fire. However, there was one promising aspect contained within the large room that had not been present in the others: books. He had stumbled into the library. He did not have long before he needed to find Matthew and leave the manor house. The discovery of this particular room suddenly seemed like a perfect gift.

As he opened the door further, and stepped into the grand library, he gazed in awe at the floor-to-ceiling shelves containing thousands of leather-bound books; each one carefully in its place in the impressive collection. Though Matthew had ordered he destroy the diaries he held, Peter was running out of time. He quickly made a decision and ran further into the enormous library, selecting the lowest shelf on one side of the vast room. He pulled out some of the larger books, leaving a sizeable gap in the shelving. He took the little black journal in his hand, wrapping its black ribbon tightly around the pages and tying it in a tight knot. He placed King Frederick's diary at the back of the shelf, flat against the back panel, and concealed it behind the volumes he had removed, hoping it would never be discovered, at least not in his lifetime.

From the floor above him he heard a sudden, ghastly shriek breaking through the silence of the night. The deathly scream accompanied the cries of frightened children and Peter shuddered at the sounds.

"Oh, no, Matthew!" he exclaimed to himself, knowing the sorrowful echoes could only mean one thing. His friend had made a dark decision.

He heard Matthew's voice calling out his name just as he realised the second diary was still lying on the floor. In his haste, he decided the concealment of this book was not so crucial. The writings in Fergal's own hand had revealed very little of his fate, from what Peter had read. He tucked it into a small gap between two red map books and ran from the room; grateful to be ending the night. Following the evening's events, he hoped never to return.

The sun was rising and they needed to be back in their homes before the villagers began to wake. It would not take long for word to reach the residents of the king's death, and they did not wish to have suspicion fall on them.

Peter found Matthew in the entrance hall, standing in front of the closed oak doors. He could see blood dripping from Matthew's sword and his heart sank as he wished they had journeyed to find the doors bolted and ended their regretful plans before they had begun.

"Queen Violet?" he asked.

"I had no choice," came Matthew's curt response.

"And the king's children?" Peter hesitantly enquired. "What of them?"

"I have not harmed the children," Matthew assured him. "They are too young to be aware of circumstances."

Peter was unsure whether to believe him and Matthew read the accusation in his eyes. "I am not a monster!" he professed.

Peter nodded, sorry to have had the thought. He looked around the hallway's many shadows for their friend.

"Where is Samuel?" he asked. "You did not fight, did you?"

"Of course not!" Matthew exclaimed. "I have sent him to redeem himself. He is journeying to find Magissa and inform her that the village has made way for her son to reign. It is the least he can do after killing the king. Even

I had not wished for that outcome and I cared little for the man."

Peter tried to stop the memory seeping into his thoughts. He was grateful to Matthew for sending Samuel to find the witch, and he sighed with relief. Samuel had always held the greatest resolve. Despite his earlier unexpected actions, he could be trusted to find Magissa, Peter was sure of it. He would find her, bring her back to Thistlewick and she would lift this terrible curse forever. Matthew's hastily conceived plan could actually result in bringing peace back to the village.

"Did you destroy the diaries?" Matthew asked as they made their way towards the giant doors.

"I could not. But rest assured they are hidden so well in the library they will never be found." Matthew looked angry, but saw outside the night fading quickly with a new sun rising.

"That will have to do," he snapped. "You had better hope they are not found while we live and breathe."

The two men marched out of the manor house and into the unrelenting snow once more. As they journeyed home, Peter smiled to himself as the hope for resolution seemed suddenly achievable.

All would be well.

Neither of the men had noticed the crying little boy atop the spiral staircase, listening to the words of his parent's killers as they disclosed their treason. He had heard the name 'Magissa' spoken of before and felt certain she had committed a dreadful act. Whatever she had done, the results had led to the past few months of misery for his family. He did not understand everything he had overheard, but he vowed to not forget a word. One day it would all make sense to him. He would ensure that the truth behind their actions, and the events leading up to them, would not stay secret forever.

It took seventeen years for Thomas to build the courage it would require. He worked on his farm each day, formulating the methods he would use to fulfil his desire for revenge. Each weekend he travelled to the village, seeking the opportunity to act. It did not take long to find Matthew, and he learned of Peter's residence several weeks later. Samuel, however, was not a noted figure in the village, living a reclusive and solitary life. But the patient determination of Thomas was soon rewarded and he saw his father's killer for the first time. The satisfaction he felt as he piled Samuel's body on top of the rotting remains of Peter and Matthew was worth every tear. They would remain in the foundations of his hay barn for eternity. It was a burial, he concluded, befitting the men who robbed him of his life.

He had confided in his dear Hazel over many years and she had instigated many aspects of his plan quite willingly. He knew her motivation came from shame. To have learnt the truth behind the curse, and seen what her sister had become, had left her brimming with a bitter resentment. She happily planted the seeds to bring about Magissa's demise.

Ending the curse entirely, however, would take a little longer.